The Powerhouse

Ann Halam was born and raised in Manchester, and after graduating from Sussex University spent some years travelling throughout South East Asia. She now lives in Brighton with her husband and son. As well as being a children's author, Ann Halam writes adult science fiction and fantasy books, as Gwyneth Jones.

Other books by the same author from Orion

The Haunting of Jessica Raven
The Fear Man

The Powerhouse

ANN HALAM

Orion Children's Books
and
Dolphin Paperbacks

For Betty Gwilliam

Acknowledgments

I'd like to thank Andy Murray, for reading the manuscript and vetting my use of modern musical terms. Also Patrick and Leon Charleton, and Gabriel Jones, who were with me on the first expedition to the mysterious building that I've called 'the Powerhouse'. Inspiration for important features of the story came from Sheridan Le Fanu's story *Green Tea*; and Robert Hugh Benson's classic novel of the macabre, *The Necromancers*.   A.H.

First published in Great Britain in 1997
as an Orion hardback
and a Dolphin paperback
by Orion Children's Books
a division of the Orion Publishing Group Ltd
Orion House
5 Upper St Martin's Lane
London WC2H 9EA

A catalogue record for this book is available
from the British Library

Typeset by Deltatype Ltd, Birkenhead, Merseyside.
Printed in Great Britain by Clays Ltd, St Ives plc

ISBN 1 85881 405 7 (hb)
ISBN 1 85881 379 4 (pb)

The Powerhouse

Introducing the team:

There were three of us, performing artists extraordinaire (that's what Jef used to put on our flyers): Me, I'm Robs, Roberta Hayward. There's nothing extraordinary about me, but it doesn't matter because I'm technical – I don't have to *perform* my part, the machines do it. Jef wrote the songs, Maddy and he came up with the melodies, I did the arrangements (I suppose you'd call it). Jef: D. Mark Jeffries (first name Darryl, but he didn't *ever* use it). Not all that tall, skinny as a spider, full of energy. Red hair in spiky corkscrews flying about all over his head, and huge green eyes. On stage he favoured jumble sale suits several sizes too small, Clark Kent horn–rimmed glasses that made his eyes look even bigger; and the lights in his red hair made it look as if his head was on fire. The girls loved him. And Maddy, Madeleine Wei Wei Turner. Wild athletic dancer, beautiful voice with an amazing range. Hair black, complexion pale, upcurved dark eyes (her mother's Singapore Chinese) nose short and straight, mouth a bit too wide, white teeth. I'm not describing her well. I don't know how to do it. But I remember her face so clearly … If Jef was touched by fire, Maddy was a flame. It wasn't just on stage, or with us. Everybody felt it. Maybe you know someone a bit like Maddy. She had everything, looks, charm, intelligence, talent. But people didn't hate her, because she didn't make you feel that she thought she was better than you. Anyone who came near could warm their hands at what Maddy was. Anyone could share her fire. There were few people who didn't smile when they were talking about Maddy, or were in her company. I'm smiling now. She was wonderful.

Note the tense, I said *was*. Note it, and then forget it, because I'm going to tell you a story.

One

IT WAS ONE OF THE LAST DAYS OF THE CHRISTMAS holiday. I was in the Wild Park with my little brother and his two best friends, Tom and Nicholas Campbell from next door. A whole gang of us had been tobogganing. But there'd hardly been enough snow. What there was left after a morning of relentless punishment had been gouged and ground up by boots and runners until it was half-frozen mud. The slope down to the goldfish pond, where we always did our tobogganing, looked like a rugby pitch with a pinball-machine tilt. It was horribly littered with bits of torn cardboard, lost gloves, scraps of bin-bag plastic. To tell you the truth, most thirteen-year-old girls don't mix well with little boys, and my so-called friends had not been a great help with the babysitting. I'd been quite glad when Stef and Maeve and DeeDee and the others had headed off in search of hot drinks, security from crazed infants with snowballs in their mitts, and other civilised comforts.

The sky was still bright blue, it was only two o'clock. Jerry (that's my brother) and I didn't want to go home. We both liked Solange, our au-pair. But we'd become slightly tired of her full-time company in the week or so since Christmas and New Year. She fussed, and though she was only nineteen she had delusions of being our nanny. On the other hand, I knew that if I had one more fistful of brown slush stuffed down my neck by the darling little boys, I was going to clock one of them really hard. So I said, 'Let's do something different. Let's be Antarctic explorers.'

Nick liked that. He was young enough to have some imagination, something little boys lose all too soon. Tom and Jerry (they loved being Tom and Jerry, like the cat and mouse in the old cartoons) put up a protest, but I wasn't having any. I told them the tobogganing was impossible, which it was; and if they scraped the slope for any more slushballs they'd be ruining their chances of tobogganing tomorrow even if it snowed all night. They were impressed by that. They think I possess secret wisdom about things like snow quality, because I'm older. I grabbed the rope and marched off, dragging our sledge.

So naturally all three of them piled onto it and started yelling 'Mush! Mush!', the way you're supposed to do to encourage husky dogs. I hauled them over a large rut, and accidentally-on-purpose tipped them off. Then I took possession of the sled and made them drag me. They seemed to like being dogs. We spent a few happy minutes zigzagging to and fro along the foot of the slope, all of us yelling 'Mush! Mush!' But as I always find when I'm babysitting Jerry, minutes is as long as any peace lasts. They started getting violent again. Menaced by more slush-attacks, I said it was time to start exploring.

The only part of the 'Wild Park' that's actually left as wilderness is a brambly hillside behind the Pagoda Café, on the other side of the goldfish pool from the toboggan slope. The coffee bar was shut up for the winter. The pool was looking extremely messy. There were Coke cans floating in melted patches, and all kinds of dead leaves and miserable slimy stubs of vegetation sticking out of the ice around the edges. The boys wanted to see if we could cross it by hopping from floe to floe, but I wouldn't let them. Sometimes I have attacks of Nanny-ness myself. We went round it and on up the hill, into the wild patch.

I must have been taken to the Wild Park hundreds, maybe thousands, of times since I was old enough to be strapped into a buggy. I'd had my first adventures on the swings and things in the playground down by the front entrance. I'd cried when they took away the old tubular helicopter and the pink plastic elephant that you could climb inside, and replaced them with those 'tasteful' giant wooden animals. I'd nagged for ices from the Pagoda Café, I'd been frightened by the wasps in the rubbish bins, I'd fallen in the pond as often as any other child in town. I'd played hide and seek in the little wilderness of brambles. But I didn't know what lay beyond.

Have you ever looked into a rock pool, and seen the shellfish creeping about? That's what I was like, a limpet on a rock. I crept a few inches one way: school. A few inches in other directions: the park, my friends' houses, the shopping centre, cinemas, music class; and I thought I knew the whole ocean. I think most people are the same. They have a set of fixed tracks that they run on every day, without ever straying. It would knock them over with shock just to take a different turning on the way to work. And maybe people are right to stick to their safe little routines. I don't know what made me leave my usual limpet-groove that day. But I know it changed my life.

When we reached the boundary wall of the Wild Park we found a gap, and a path leading into a sort of scrubby unclaimed wood. I climbed on the wall and had a look around. I was amazed to see the big windows of my school winking in the sunlight, on the hillside up above the trees. 'This the North West Passage,' I said. 'We're going to find out if we can reach Montrose Road (the road my school, West Bradfield Comprehensive, was on) by the unmapped wilderness route.'

We tried to climb the hill. It was fun in a way, except that people had been dumping rubbish among the trees, so you had to watch out for traps of rusty metal hidden under the pretty white snow. Eventually Tom fell all the way to the bottom, with the sledge on top of him. He wasn't much hurt, but he was depressed because his new Arsenal tracksuit trousers had taken a battering. We rubbed him down as best we could, and decided to see where the path would take us. It was very overgrown. The branches of the trees met overhead, and tall weeds poked through the snow crust. It felt spooky. I speak with hindsight, but I really do remember that afternoon: how cold the air was, how it tasted of smoke and frost. It felt as if we'd somehow slipped out of our familar world into the unknown, into untrodden wastes beyond our knowledge … I was enjoying myself. Being with the boys gave me an excuse to make-believe, without worrying about having to act like a proper, cynical teenage girl.

The path lead us to an open space. Suddenly, there was a building in front of us. It was an odd, ugly, chunky blockhouse, built of glossy orange brick. It had rows of tall, round-arched windows and a kind of domed roof. We stood in the snow, amazed. I'd never seen this place in my life before. I couldn't imagine what it was doing here, in the middle of the woods. I even wondered for a moment if I was dreaming. It looked so mysterious, so *important* – and yet it had no purpose that I could make out.

'What should we do?' whispered Tom. As if the building could hear us; and as if it posed a problem that we had to solve.

It couldn't ever have been a private house. It looked more like maybe a library, an old-fashioned swimming pool, a very small old hospital. It had that kind of pompous, public works, Victorian look. But it seemed to be derelict. There were big gaps in the high mesh fence that had once surrounded the forecourt in which we were standing, where black gritty cinder showed through the thin snow. We hadn't noticed the fence when we passed through because the part by the path through the trees was completely collapsed. In the front it was still upright and there were gates, but they were wide open. A track seemed to lead down to the road that went past the Wild Park. The snow was mashed up by ruts and tyre marks, showing that travellers, or tramps maybe, had used the site; and there was a small, dirty white caravan standing beside some tumbledown outbuildings. But there was no one about now.

'Let's see if we can get inside.'

I didn't think we'd be able to get in. I was wrong. The big double doors had once been padlocked shut, but someone had broken in before us, cutting through the rusty chain that had held the padlock. The doors stood ajar.

'Wow!' breathed Jerry, peering inside. 'WEIRD!'

I was expecting to hear someone yell: *Hey, what are you kids doing?*

No one yelled. We were alone.

'*What's it for?*' demanded Jerry, whispering again.

What was inside the double doors wasn't *outstandingly* weird. There were no monsters, no corpses, no aliens from outer space. But it was strange. In front of us there was one huge room that went up to the domed roof; with a big wide stage at the far end, reached by a flight of stone steps. The lower floor was concrete, scattered with all kinds of rubbish: rags and old half bricks, food cartons and bits of deceased furniture. We could see clearly, because lots of light came in through those arched windows. Up in the roof, under the dome, there were tracks running from wall to wall. A massive metal hook still dangled from a steel hawser on a pulley wheel, and loops of the cable lay across the floor. On the other side of the hall, to our right, there was a doorway without a door leading to shadowy smaller rooms.

'Maybe it's something to do with power supply,' I said, after staring for a moment. 'It could be an ancient substation.'

'Somewhere where they used to store electricity?'

'You can't store electricity. A substation is where they step down the voltage of the current that comes from the power station, so it's safe for domestic use.'

I'd done some project work on electricity in school, I suppose that was why the idea came to me. Or perhaps it was because the place felt as if it had *power* ... even then. 'If it's a powerhouse,' I went on, looking around. 'There should be some great big transformers.' But except for that huge hook, whatever fittings or machinery there had been in here had been stripped out long ago.

Jerry had lost interest. My brother had a habit of asking me questions, the way bright, inquisitive children are supposed to do, to show their intelligence: and then never listening to what I had to say. I think he resented the way I always knew the answers (if I didn't, I made something up: essential big-sister self defence). He and Tom and Nicky barged past me, into the big hall.

I found out later that the building I called a powerhouse had been a water pumping station. Yet I was right in a way, because there *was* a kind of power in there. A power stored, in spite of what I'd said to Jerry. A charge built up, and waiting hungrily for release ... But that first moment as I stood gazing, taking it all in, I didn't sense any danger. My powerhouse – already the name felt as if it belonged – was a wonderful, spooky mystery. I wanted it to have been built by aliens; or by a secret government department, for some bizarre purpose no one was ever supposed to discover. It wasn't hard to imagine some kind of Frankenstein's laboratory: a big platform on scaffolding cranked up under the dome, lightning bolts flashing down those steel cables. I wondered how long it had been standing empty and open. There were paint-ings on the white tiles of the lower walls that obviously didn't belong to its industrial past. I saw faded giant daisy flowers, clouds, a rayed sun. I thought maybe they'd been done by the travellers who lived in the white caravan. But it was surprising how little the building had been vandalised. None of the windows were broken.

We kicked through the rubbish on the floor, and found some peculiar remnants that looked like old stage props: a branch of a tree, made of chickenwire and painted papier-mâché; a length of stained black velvet, a carousel horse without a head. There was a door in the wall under the stage that was still locked. The boys rattled and banged at it in vain. Then they decided to explore the rooms beyond the empty doorway in the right hand wall. I went with them far enough to see that there wasn't much trouble they could get into, and came back to the hall. That bare arena fascinated me. It gave me an odd feeling, a prickly, *something's going to happen* excitement. I was thinking how Maddy and Jef would love this place.

Maddy Turner and Jef Jeffries were three years older than me and in their last year at school. They'd been playing rock music – a special kind of rock music, electronic sound and linked visuals – for ages. First they'd played with Jef's big brother John. But John, who was the technical wizard, had finished at Bradfield Art College, moved to Manchester and joined a different band. Maddy and Jef had advertised for a replacement, and they'd got me. We were *Hajetu*, a techno-art music performance group. *Hajetu* was the first syllables of our three surnames. We were using it until we thought of something better. But perhaps we never would. It seemed to work. It sounded like a word in an unknown language. People could read different meanings into it – and that suited our act.

I'd been with them since October. Those three months had been without question the happiest time of my life. My parents weren't too pleased. They wanted me to be a concert pianist, practising ten hours a day and resting quietly with some homework in my spare time. They hated the whole idea of *Hajetu*. But I was in heaven. I loved the machines: the sound-to-light units John Jeffries had built at college, that translated our music into bright swirling colour. I loved our intense rehearsals. I loved working out new ideas. Most of all, I loved being with Maddy and Jef. Especially Maddy. Jef, as was generally agreed by everyone including himself, could be a pain. But Maddy was always kind. I admired her so much, I couldn't believe my luck at having her for an actual friend.

If you are what is called 'talented', and it stands out enough to be noticed when you're very young, you do not get much time to be a normal person. From when I was about seven, whatever anyone else was doing, you could bet that I was playing the piano. Or the clarinet, my second instrument. Or else I was writing music, or experimenting (eventually) on the first keyboard sampler I blackmailed my parents into buying for me. (It was easy. I said *if you don't, I'll be so depressed I won't be able to practise*). They were always fairly willing to buy me things, it was a shame I didn't want more 'things', really. I'm not complaining. I loved my music, and I was used to the grind. But it did make me different. Though I had friends my own age to hang out with, I never felt completely at home with them. I felt as if I was speaking a foreign language that I didn't know well, and at any minute I might make some ridiculous, embarrassing mistake. With Maddy and Jef I didn't have to worry. They were three years older. I wasn't *supposed* to understand them. I could relax and enjoy their company, and our music.

I had a closer look at the grimy wall paintings. I picked over the odd rubbish. But the stone stage kept drawing my eyes. Finally I gave in to temptation. I climbed up the steps on to that wide empty platform. I was holding a little toy windmill on a stick, the sort of thing you can buy at the seaside. It had a rusty rivet in the centre and sails of dust-crusted purple and yellow plastic. I could hear the boys shouting cheerfully at each other, somewhere out of sight. Their voices raised flat, deadened echoes in the dome. I noticed that the acoustic wasn't very good. But you can do anything with sound, if you have the right machines.

The one thing I didn't enjoy about *Hajetu* was the performing. I'd done plenty of performing on my own, of course: but that was with a great big piano to hide behind; and in front of me only the examiner for a grade exam, or a quiet, sedate audience of Mums and Dads. With *Hajetu* I'd only done two gigs so far, but I'd found them very different from what I was used to. Everything was rowdy, noisy and confused, and it scared me.

However, there was no audience now. I took a quick glance round to make sure the little boys weren't coming back. I held up my decrepit seaside windmill (we didn't often use hand-held mikes, but it's traditional for occasions like this). I sang into it: one of my favourite *Hajetu* songs; and I began to dance. I was pretending to be Maddy. I loved watching her in action, though when we were doing our stuff I only saw her from the back. She would jump in the air and fly, swirl around like a Catherine wheel, the colours of the music spiralling around her, soaring and swooping with her marvellous voice …

It was a terrific great big space. The floor was solid and had no spring, but I didn't mind that. I was completely carried away. My useful anorak and fleecy-lined black jogging bottoms had become Maddy's dragonfly-dress, the one with all the little rainbow lights. I tossed my head as if I had Maddy's long black hair, instead of my own sensible crop …

Then I stepped into something.

Have you ever been frightened? I mean really *frightened*, suddenly, for no reason, in some ordinary place? You soon realised there was nothing to be scared of, I'm sure. But think of that moment. Hold it in your mind. That's what happened to me.

Sometimes I feel normal and ordinary. Sometimes I feel as if I stick out like a sore thumb. I stare into the mirror in the morning and I despise myself. I think I'm the most worthless person in the world, and I hate everyone. Do you know the feeling? You probably do. Most people have times like that. It's horrible but it doesn't last. Imagine suddenly feeling full of that total self-digust. Imagine being overwhelmed, without warning, by the most horrible hateful emotions. That was what was waiting for me, up on the stage in the Powerhouse. And it wasn't just me feeling bad. *I wasn't alone.* There was something inside me, a maggot in my brain. It was feeding on all the evil in me, all the secret misery, and squeezing me for more …

I had never, never been so frightened.

I don't know how it ended. I was dancing about, this thing happened to my brain: then it was over as suddenly as it had begun.

'Robs? What are you doing? What's wrong?'

I was crouching on the huge dusty stage. Winter sunlight was pouring into the derelict hall, and three little boys were standing down there staring up at me. I was on my knees. I think I'd been clutching my head in my hands: no wonder they looked worried.

'Did I scream?'

Jerry shook his head. 'You sort of moaned. What happened?'

I thought I saw something move, low down on the floor beside me: a flicker of darkness. It was like some small scurrying animal, glimpsed out of the corner of my eye. Next moment there was nothing. From the empty space I felt a breath of horrible cold air. It wasn't warm in the Powerhouse, but this was different: a dank, icy presence, nothing like the crisp dry chill of a winter's day.

I was determined not to lose it in front of the kids. It was partly big-sister pride, and partly that I knew I had to protect them. If Jerry were to come up here. If he were to feel what I had just felt … I couldn't stand the idea.

'I saw a rat,' I gasped. I swallowed hard. 'Big rat. It startled me.'

My darling brother jeered loudly.

'You were scared of one measly rat? Let me up there. Let's have a hunt!'

I got to my feet. My legs were shaking. But I felt better the moment I'd taken a step away from that unpleasant cold spot. 'No.' I said firmly. 'Don't come up here. It's time we were getting back. And you're dirty enough already.' It was true, all three boys were now horribly filthy, even Tom in his beloved Arsenal kit.

Tom and Nicolas were not keen on rats. They were easily persuaded to leave the hunt for another day, and I think Jerry was secretly relieved. We went outside. They discussed coming back with torches to explore the rooms that had been too dark for them: bringing food, making a den. We argued about whose fault it was that we'd brought no rations on our polar trek. Then we spent some time trying to remember where we'd left the sledge. Eventually we found it and went home.

I don't know if this will make any sense, but though I'd been completely terrified up on the stage in the Powerhouse, I didn't *stay* frightened. The fear was up on that stone stage, I didn't take it away with me. I don't mean I forgot what had happened. I remember recalling something about 'cold patches' in haunted houses. I remember wondering if the Powerhouse was haunted. But I'm not the sort of person who gets spooked easily. My strange bad moment could have come from inside myself. It could have been indigestion, for all I knew. Before we got home I was making plans (though I didn't tell the boys) to come back with Jef and Maddy, and show off my extraordinary find.

Solange squawked like a mad hen over the state Jerry was in. But she was okay about it, and made sure there were no traces before Mum or Dad got home from work.

ii

I was very nervous on the first day back at school. Nothing to do with school work, or reforming those alliances with friends your own age that always get a bit skewed over the holidays. I wasn't worried about any of that. My problem was that I didn't know what was happening about *Hajetu*. We hadn't been planning to rehearse over Christmas and New Year. But I'd been expecting one or other of them to contact me, and they hadn't. I was afraid they'd decided that having me in the band was a horrible mistake.

You see, Maddy and Jef had advertised in school at the beginning of the autumn term for someone to take over the synths and the mixing desk. I thought it was a school thing, so I'd answered the advertisment. I'd never have dared if I'd known they were advertising in real music papers as well. They'd been very surprised, because I was so young. I'd been surprised too. I'd been playing with various kinds of electronic keyboards and samplers whenever I got the chance for years. But I'd never seen anything like the Gesture Wall, or the Very Nervous System. Or Maddy's Techno-Colour Hipster belt; or the Dragonfly-Dress; or Jef's Mind-Burst Platforms Souls. All of these things were prototypes, instruments Jef's brother had made at college. The Wall and the System were stage furniture that plugged into my desk. Jef and

Maddy wore the other things. They were all ways of getting special effects: sound and movement turned into waves and showers of coloured light. Anyway, Jef and Maddy had taken me on, and it had seemed to work. But I still felt I was on trial. Not getting a call had thrown me. They were so much older. I hadn't had the courage to ring up one of them and ask what was going on.

When I saw Maddy and Jef standing together in the lower school reception area at lunchtime, I didn't know whether to go up to them or creep by. Luckily, Maddy saw me.

'Robs,' she cried. 'We've been hunting for you.'

'I'm intensely sorry,' broke in Jef dramatically. 'One of us should have called you. But we only knew today that there was no hope. We have terrible news.'

I could feel my face going hot and cold by turns. Maybe I'd broken one of the machines, done something awful to it when I was playing around at our last session.

'W-what's wrong?' I managed to stutter.

He groaned. '*The shed is gone,*' he declared, in hollow tones.

The shed was an old craft and technology workshop in a prefab, that had been abandoned because it was too damp to be used even as a store room. It wasn't much more than a big garage with a power supply. It leaked and the roof wasn't safe. The school had been threatening to bulldoze it for ages. Meanwhile we'd been using it for free two evenings a week, as a rehearsal space. But we'd known this couldn't last.

'Oh,' I blurted out, before I could stop myself, 'is that all?'

Jef looked astounded. 'All?' he demanded furiously. 'What do you mean, *is that all*? Do you have a fully equipped music studio in your house that we can use? Do you even know where there's an empty garage? Maybe we can find a disused hut up on the allotments.'

The hordes were thundering by, heading for second sitting in the canteen (actually the Lower School assembly hall). Jef was getting so loud by the end of this speech you could hear him clear above the din. Passing teachers gave him ominous looks.

'She means nobody's *died*, dummy,' Maddy told him, jabbing her elbow in his ribs. 'Nobody's dead, or even sick. We haven't lost our voices or broken any limbs, and your brother hasn't reclaimed the machines. We'll work something out.'

We went to walk around the playing fields, where Jef could yell and wave his arms as the mood inspired him, without getting us moved on by the corridor police. Gradually, I realised that this really was a disaster. We needed space, we needed a power supply, we needed a sound system that we could plug our customised machines into. We'd had all these things. Now they were gone.

'Couldn't you ask Mr Briggs?' I dared to suggest.

Mr Briggs was the head of our Art Department. He wasn't the head of Music, but he had an iron grip on anything to do with what he called 'The Creative Arts', in school. He was the one who doled out time-slots in the normal music practice rooms. Unfortunately he hated Jef. He'd hated John Jeffries too. I'd never had much to do with Mr Briggs, but he had a reputation for being pompous and sarcastic, always putting people down. John Jeffries had been brilliant at art, and Jef was the same, but neither of them was the sort to respond well to that kind of treatment. Jef's naturally white skin turned bright red, and his permanent freckles stood out like chickenpox. He tugged at his ragged string of a school tie.

'I *have*,' he snapped. 'This morning, when I found the shed was gone. I went and begged for a space. I said pretty-please. I was *polite*. He turned me down flat.'

Maddy and I exchanged a hopeless glance. We could imagine the mess Jef would have made of being 'polite' to a teacher he hated.

'The practice rooms are too small anyway,' said Maddy. 'We'd need the drama studio, or one of the halls. And they're booked out.'

West Bradfield was a Community School. When we went home it had a second life, full of adults doing craft courses, learning Italian and rehearsing plays.

We'd reached the demolition site. We stared at the blank muddy space where *Hajetu's* home had stood. It had been the last of the old prefabs. Now that it was gone, a whole unused stretch of campus was free for new development.

'Maybe they'll build something worthwhile,' suggested Maddy, looking on the bright side. 'The shed *was* a bit of an eyesore.'

'Ah, Darryl, Maddy.'

It was Mr Briggs himself. He was a hearty blue-eyed blond, a middle-aged natty dresser who thought he was still a bit of a hunk. But he was beginning to have a belly, and his hair was getting thin on top. He had a fatal habit of stroking his hand over his head, as if feeling to make sure no more had fallen off since he last checked. He was waving a wad of what looked like raffle tickets.

'You three young performing stars,' he smirked, making the word 'stars' purely sarcastic, 'will be interested in this. I have some complimentary passes to give away, and that means free. I'm sure you can come along to the Gallery this evening, to greet the town's new Artist in Residence. As you would know, if you paid attention in Assembly this morning, we have a nationally important artist coming to Bradfield.'

He must have known how we felt about the shed. He knew all about *Hajetu*. He glanced from Jef to the cleared site with a smug little smile.

'I see you're admiring the new car park. Or what will be the new car park, once we get the tarmac laid. I agree, the loss of that useless old shack is a great improvement. Now, come on. Only a few tickets left.'

Maddy said, 'Thanks Mr Briggs, but we're busy this evening.'

'I don't give a toss for your Artist in Residence,' snarled Jef. He passed a hand over his red curls, in exactly Mr Briggs' famous gesture. His other hand was perched insolently on his hip. 'I'm an artist myself, I don't have to get anyone to do it for me. I don't have to grovel before some *nationally important* time waster.'

Briggs didn't bawl Jef out for insolence. He just shrugged and put his tickets away. 'It's your loss, my young friends.' He surveyed the site once more, 'A much better use of the space,' he remarked, grinning, and strolled away.

When he'd gone, Jef started ranting and raving, claiming Briggs had personally arranged to have the shed demolished just to spite *Hajetu*, and he'd deliberately come over with those stupid tickets to gloat over our despair. Maddy tried to calm him, but in the end he rushed away, calling 'Don't follow me! I want to be alone!'

'Poor Jef,' Maddy sighed. 'It must have cost him to ask Briggs for anything. But I wish he'd let me try, first. I might have wangled something. Too late now.'

I remembered the first time I'd met Maddy. My parents had fought to get me into West Bradfield because of the school's music facilities, though it wasn't our nearest school at all. I hadn't moved up with anyone from my primary school, and I knew I was going to be useless at making friends. I was huddled on the floor in the girls' toilets by the Reception Area one day in my first week, feeling totally miserable. Maddy came in: a tall girl with lots of black curly hair, short skirt, long elegant legs.

— 18 —

She came and asked me was I okay. I told her my cat had died, to explain why I was crying. She sat down next to me on the floor and talked as if we'd known each other for ages: about the school, about different teachers and how to handle them, and all the little wrinkles you need to know to get by in a new place ... I thought she was just making conversation, and I wished I could chatter as easily as that. I realised afterwards that she'd given me exactly what I needed: information, things that other Year Sevens wanted to know, things that would help me to make friends. That was Maddy, typical Maddy. I bet she knew I'd never owned a cat in my life, too.

I'm sure she'd forgotten this incident long ago, but I hadn't. It was partly because I remembered the day she'd rescued me that I'd plucked up the courage to answer *Hajetu*'s advertisement; and suddenly become the friend and colleague of the two most interesting, most exciting people in school. It had been like a dream, and now it was over. I was sure it was over. Maddy and Jef would find some way to carry on. But whatever they did couldn't happen at school, because of Jef's feud with Mr Briggs. So it wouldn't include me.

'What's this about an Artist in Residence?' I asked, to fill the silence.

'It's the Free Trade Art Gallery, in town,' replied Maddy. 'It was in Senior Assembly this morning. You'll probably hear about in yours.' (Junior Assembly was in the afternoon.) 'They're having an Artist in Residence. She's going to be working on projects with all the schools, and then there'll be an exhibition in the festival. She's a Roman Catholic nun, or an ex-nun or something. She's called Sister Dominic Mary, but her civilian name is Kathleen Dunne. She's quite famous, I think. I vaguely remember seeing something about her on TV, but I can't remember what.'

'What kind of art does a nun do?'

'No idea. I wasn't listening. Embroidery, maybe. Rich embroidery on vestments.'

'Stained glass?'

'Illuminated prayer books?' Maddy shrugged. 'Poor old Briggs. Did you see that great wad of tickets? The great and good of Bradfield must be in a panic, because nobody's going to be there to meet and greet their Nationally Important Artist. But we can't help out. We have to go and talk to Dave Ramsey. He's our only hope. We're going down to his studio after school. You have to come too. We ought to all talk to him together.'

I felt my cheeks getting hot, this time with relief and pleasure. I wasn't going to be shut out, not straight away. 'I'll have to call Solange,' I muttered.

Dave Ramsey ran a rehearsal studio, down in the funky part of town. Jef and Maddy knew him because of Jef's brother. He'd helped us a lot. John Jeffries had been famous, on the scale of things in our town. It was certainly because of John that Dave had been able to get bookings for us (all two of them, so far), even though we were so young, and our act so strange compared to the usual cheesy old rock and roll you got in Bradfield's less select music venues. When we went down to the Heavy Heart studio that afternoon, I think we were half-sure that he would pull us out of this mess too.

But he couldn't.

We told him our sad tale, in the front office – a bare room that had been a corner shop, where an overstuffed purple sofa stood in the window, flanked by big black boxes and reels of cable; and Dave's big desk was a teetering pile of papers. He shook his head.

'I'm sorry kids,' he said, 'I can't help you. I've some building work on, fixing my dry rot. I'm down to one studio and I just do not have a slot.'

'We couldn't take it,' said Maddy, firmly. 'You can't

afford to give your space away. That's not why we came. We don't know what to do, we hoped you might have some ideas.'

Rehearsal space at the Heavy Heart was fifteen pounds a session. I knew this (I'd never thought about it before) because I was reading it on the list of terms pinned up on Dave's cluttered noticeboard. If we went down to one rehearsal a week … Fifteen pounds didn't sound like a huge amount. I knew that Maddy and Jef didn't have any money. They didn't have time for part-time jobs, between schoolwork and *Hajetu*; and of course we didn't get paid for our gigs. (You must be kidding. The landlords at our venues definitely thought *we* should be paying *them*). I didn't have any money either, but I could probably squeeze it out of my parents. Maddy and Jef looked despairing. Dave Ramsey, who was a big tall black bloke, with a mass of greying dreadlocks that he generally wore tied up on top of his head, leaned back in his tatty office chair and brooded: obviously feeling bad about throwing us orphans out into the storm. I sat there, hiding my too-clean hands with their close-clipped pianist's nails, feeling horribly aware of my sensible haircut and my sensible clothes. Dave's desk was piled with little stacks of flyers, all the colours of the rainbow, for every act at every music venue for miles around. I wondered if I dared to say that I could raise the money. It seemed such a cheek. I was the junior one, the outsider. It would be as if I was trying to *buy* my place in their world. Luckily Dave put me out of my misery.

'I wouldn't take your money. You can use any free slot that comes along, and pay me back when you're rich and famous. But I genuinely don't *have* any room, not right now.'

A thought suddenly came into my mind. It was ridiculous. The place was derelict. It had no power supply. But if Dave would have a space soon, it would only be for a few weeks. There was a stage, an enormous stage: and plenty of light as long as it was daytime …

'This is probably a really stupid idea …' I began. They all looked at me. I felt myself blushing. 'But I found somewhere. A derelict building. A big, empty space. I think it used to be an electricity station or something. It's probably no use, but it might be worth looking.'

Dave sat up. 'An empty building? Where?'

I described the Powerhouse, how it looked and where it stood, lost in that scrubby patch of woodland beyond the Wild Park.

The big man listened, and he nodded. '*That* place? Yes, I know it, knew it long ago.' He seemed about to say something more. In that moment, while he hesitated, I remembered the cold spot. I was going to say something about it … But it seemed so stupid. Then Dave shrugged, as if deciding we wouldn't be interested in his reminiscences. '*That* place,' he repeated (and the moment when I might have told them was gone). 'So you found *that* place. I suppose, if it's still standing, and you say there's no locks on the doors, it could be all right. Maybe we could rig something up. Just for a few weeks, there'd be no harm.'

'Well, okay,' shouted Jef, jumping up from the sofa. 'What are we waiting for? Let's go see!'

So that was it. Dave drove us to the Wild Park in his saggy old white Cortina with the peeling Pink Panther decals. He seemed to know the way. He drove right up the track through the woods, into the cindery forecourt. The Powerhouse loomed there, just as I remembered it. As far as I could tell, everything was as it had been the week before. It was dark by this time. We three piled out of the car. Dave stayed behind the wheel.

There it stood, ugly and chunky and solid.

'Cool!' said Jef.

'I'd no idea … ' breathed Maddy. '*How strange.* I've been in the Wild Park so many times, and never known this was here. How spooky!'

I felt warmed by the thought that Maddy had exactly the same reaction as I'd had.

The white caravan was gone. I had a sort of feeling the forecourt was different, that there were lumps and heaps lying about that I didn't remember. But it was difficult to see much. The double doors were standing ajar, just as they'd been before. Jef stepped inside, and whistled, raising a faint breathy echo in the big domed space. He groped the wall by the doors, automatically searching for a light switch. To my immense surprise there was a click, and then a fusillade of clicks. He'd found a bank of switches that I had never even noticed. A row of lights came on: bright white bulbs in old-fashioned sconces along the walls.

I saw something I thought was a rat, sitting boldly upright in the middle of the floor. But it whisked away instantly, a flicker of darkness.

'Ace!' Jef crowed. 'I thought you said it didn't have power. This is perfect!'

'Fantastic,' breathed Maddy. 'Totally fantastic!'

Dave tooted his horn. He'd warned us that he was in a hurry.

'We'd better go,' grinned Maddy. 'But we'll be back.'

'We'll be squatters,' declared Jef. 'We'll change the locks, fix the place up. Did you see that *hook*? And the stage, the size of it! It'll be intense.'

I was amazed at how quickly it had happened. I knew there were things I ought to say, things I ought to have told them. But it seemed to be too late.

Two

THERE WAS A DELAY AFTER THAT. WE NEEDED transport to get our stuff (which was being stored in John Jeffries' empty bedroom at Jef's house) over to the Powerhouse. We needed Dave to help us move in; and he didn't have the time. We gave Jef the job of going past the Powerhouse regularly, to make sure no one came and locked it up or suddenly decided to knock it down. And we relaxed a little, hoping that the crisis was over. We discussed finding out who owned the building and trying to get permission to use it. But we decided that if we started on that trail, we'd never get anywhere. We only wanted to use the Powerhouse for a few weeks. If someone came along and evicted us, we'd just go quietly. We also wanted to make it clear to whoever was concerned that we were willing to pay for the power we used. We all thought that using a derelict building was all right, but not paying for the electricity sounded criminal. Dave said he knew how to sort that side of it out. Obviously he was still feeling responsible for us. He couldn't have been nicer … except that he somehow didn't have a free moment to drive us and the stuff around there. I did have a *slight* suspicion that he didn't really like the plan, and was hoping we'd go off it, or that he'd find us another space. But if that was true, it didn't work out: and two weeks later, he said he could move us in.

We arrived at the Powerhouse about eleven o'clock on

a Saturday morning. We all climbed out of the van in the forecourt. The snow was gone and it was daylight. Of course, I told myself, it wasn't surprising if everything looked very different. I stared around, trying to see the littered ground that I remembered. Everything seemed much cleaner and brighter. I assumed my imagination had made the Powerhouse seem more sinister and neglected in memory than it had been in real life. We unloaded our boxes and humped everything inside. Jef and Maddy and I were terrified that the place would turn out to be impossible. We'd been saying this all the way, in the van. Maybe that was why we didn't even glance at the hall, until we had the last case indoors.

Then we stood and stared. Winter daylight was flooding through the tall windows. The concrete floor of the main room was clean and bare. There was a door in the right hand wall, where I was sure I remembered an empty doorway. The tiled walls were gleaming, even the mysterious old industrial fittings up in the roof looked bright. On the stage, that splendid empty stage, there were several big canvas-swathed lumps.

'Someone's cleaned the windows,' I said blankly.

'The place is certainly in good shape,' remarked Dave, sounding puzzled. He'd brought in his toolbox, and a new padlock and chain. He was going to check out what kind of new lock we needed. The padlock was to keep the building secure, until he had a chance to fit it. None of the others had seen the derelict Powerhouse the way it was. Maddy and Jef had had a brief glimpse, that evening when we came in the dark. I was the only one who knew what it had been like. I was trying desperately to tell myself I was exaggerating the changes.

Then we all saw the woman. She was sitting on the floor, with her back against the wall under the stage. She was in full view but we hadn't noticed her because she was sitting so still. She was middle-aged and dumpy, with short, rough grey hair and a scoured, red-cheeked outdoor complexion. She was wearing a strange baggy off-white coat, that was wrapped tightly round her middle and came half-way to her ankles. She had unusually blue eyes. I noticed that. It's quite rare that you spot the colour of someone's eyes the first time you meet them. These were very bright: maybe it was the contrast with those red cheeks. We all thought she was a tramp.

Jef, startled, jumped straight into the attack. 'What are you doing in here, Missus?'

Maddy added, in a much nicer voice, 'Is something wrong? Can we help?'

I muttered, looking round worriedly, '*Everything's different –*'

The dumpy woman said, '*Everything has changed, changed utterly. A terrible beauty is born.* I don't see the terrible beauty yet. I'm trying hard.' She grinned, as if she'd made a joke. She had an Irish accent.

At that moment, a horrendous, almost psychic suspicion came into my head. But before I could speak, a lot more things happened at once. Several vehicles drove up outside the Powerhouse. There was a burst of chattering and footsteps. Dave, with his toolbox and his padlock, barely had time to dodge out of the way as a pile of people walked in through the open doors. In the first rank was a short, squat man in an expensive business suit with a thick gold chain draped across his chest. On one side of him was a thin, well-dressed woman in apple-green, with upswept hair and dangly earrings. On the other was our own Mr Briggs, in his smartest clothes; the remains of his blond hair carefully arranged. Behind them were some more people wearing their best clothes, plus three young men and a young woman all in black leather jackets, wearing professional cameras slung round their necks and clutching tape-recorders. Behind *them* came a couple of other people who looked like teachers, also dressed up smartly, and a whole crowd of little girls and boys about Jerry's age, all of them clutching clipboards and pencil-cases.

We stared at this invading horde. They stared at us. They saw two whackily dressed teenagers and serious-looking girl in very ordinary clothes (that's me); plus a huge man with a bundle of dreadlocks tied on top of his head, wearing a shaggy jacket that seemed to be made of acid-yellow polar bear fur, and brandishing a length of heavy-duty chain. That was Dave. Jef, when he isn't at school or dressed up as Clark Kent, likes the kind of clothes that make *Big-Issue* vendors smile at him kindly and wave him by. Maddy was wearing jazz patterned tights, an antique (I mean second-hand) purple suede miniskirt, and her most shrunken fluffy sweater, under a fringed and studded suede cowboy jacket that came nearly to her knees. We must have looked like a circus act. I think the people saw Dave mostly, at first, because they all seemed to take a step backwards. The woman in apple-green recovered first. 'Ah, the workmen are still here,' she announced brightly. 'I'm afraid we *have* arrived a little early. You people carry on setting up.' She waved a hand at us, graciously. 'We'll take a short tour of the premises.'

I had recognised the squat man. It was the Lord Mayor of Bradfield, Harry Steel. I'd seen his picture in the local paper. He was short but not small, he looked as if he'd been meant to be pretty big, but something had squashed him. His face was red, and creased like a pug-dog's. But he didn't look a bad sort.

'Workmen?' he repeated dubiously, beetling his bushy eyebrows at me and Maddy and Jef and Dave. It wasn't a very likely description. I wondered, desperately, what we were supposed to be setting up, and how we could pretend to be doing it.

One of the teachers could be heard to whisper, 'But there's nothing *here!*'

Jef was the first of us four to come unparalysed. I don't know what he thought was going on, but apparently he made up his mind to follow the apple-green lady's instructions, in his own way. He went over to one of our cases, without saying a word to anyone, opened it and began setting up the Gesture Wall.

Then Mr Briggs exploded.

'You!' he yelled, stabbing his finger at Jef. 'OUT! Get out!' He glared at me and Maddy. 'And you two. Out of here this instant!' His face was going crimson. 'How dare you disrupt a civic occasion like this. I've had enough of your filthy bad manners, Darryl Jeffries –' Suddenly, he seemed to remember that he had an audience. He turned to the poker-faced Mayor, trying to slick a big greasy smile over his own furious features.

'I'm terribly sorry, Lord Mayor,' he oozed. 'There seems to be a misunderstanding. I'll sort it out – I know these young people.'

Warily he checked out big Dave, who was standing there amazed, then dodged past him and grabbed Jef by the elbow. I heard him muttering fiercely: 'I don't know what kind of practical joke you're planning Darryl, but it's not on! This is an important day for me, a private reception and this time you were not invited. Take your friends and get out of here –'

The group of children was beginning to fray at the edges. Seven year olds in ones and twos were sliding out of the invisible corral their teachers had thrown up around them, and escaping into the unknown. The press photographers, hoping for some exciting violence, were dead interested in what was going on between Mr Briggs and Jef. The woman in apple-green had been distracted by another wave of invaders. Several men in overalls, and another posse of people, mostly women, in black waitress dresses under their outdoor coats, had appeared at the open doors. She'd rushed over to deal with them. Mr

Briggs was mouthing off at Jef, the Lord Mayor was standing by looking amused and calm, the rest of the official guests were huddling like a flock of badly-worried sheep …

Maddy and I were standing there, completely bewildered. Or rather, I wished I *was* completely bewildered. But I was remembering things I'd vaguely heard or read: about the new, customised, redeveloped arts centre where the famous Artist in Residence was going to work. About delays in the refurbishment, and problems with the builders. I even remembered how the Artist In Residence Reception that Mr Briggs had been touting, had been postponed at the last minute. I remembered Jef cackling when he found out about this. *'Nun cancelled due to lack of interest!'* Everything was crashing down around me. The dumpy woman, who hadn't spoken since she made that strange remark about terrible beauty, was no longer sitting on the floor. She was on her feet, watching the proceedings with her mild, bright blue eyes. I saw that she didn't really look like a tramp, and that what we'd taken for a peculiar old homeless person's coat was actually a very clean and practical-looking artist's overall.

This building had been empty. It had probably been padlocked, empty and derelict for years and years. But that day when I came by with the little boys, the doors had been open. We must have arrived when the workmen had left the site for a break. The same thing must have happened when I'd come back at nightfall, the next time, with Maddy and Jef. They must have been working overtime, because they were so far behind schedule. I understood everything now. The open doors, the reconnected power supply, the way the windows weren't broken. It had been awful, awful luck that we had not known what was going on. The Powerhouse still didn't look a lot like a spanking new, customised art centre. But that was what it had to be. And our 'tramp' had to be the nationally important Sister Dominic Mary Kathleen Dunne.

Somebody had had the same idea as us. They were turning the Powerhouse into a studio and performance space, and we had gatecrashed the grand opening.

Maddy and I looked at each other, each of us with the same horrified expression. I knew that she had guessed the truth too. I still didn't understand why the famous Artist in Residence was being installed when the transformation was so far from complete. I couldn't see this as the ideal spot for embroidery workshops. But I had the general idea. I felt so stupid. I wanted to lie down and die.

The woman in apple-green had sent the waitresses and workmen around the back. She returned to her post, smiling sweetly but with panic in her eyes. Sensibly deciding not to mess with Mr Briggs and Jef, who were hissing at each other like mad snakes, she led the long-suffering Mayor and the rest of the crew away from the fight, airily pointing out the non-existent features of the new art centre.

'A coffee bar,' she explained, waving her hand over the empty hall as if she was a fairy godmother (but nothing happened). 'Ah … eventually. Kitchens behind. An exhibiton space. The gift shop.' She pointed to the door in the right-hand wall. 'Seminar rooms, small craft workshops and, er, the usual offices. Up above we have this splendid studio area, which will double as a perfomance space. I'm *very* happy. Everything has turned out so well. Imaginative development, using our industrial past.' In the midst of my own disaster I felt sorry for that lady in apple-green. I admired her for forging on. I'd had piano experiences like this tour of hers. I knew the terrible feeling when everything falls apart, and you're frantically trying to paper over the chasms. But I was much more interested in my own catastophe. All I wanted to do was get away from here, and start trying to forget about my disastrous bright idea. If only we could separate Jef from Mr Briggs without a total explosion.

I stared up into the roof, where that splendid Frankenstein pulley contraption had so far survived the remodelling. Through my despairing misery I noticed something small and dark, moving along the cable. It must be my old friend the rat. I watched it, wondering with awful fascination what would happen if a rat fell down, and landed on the Lord Mayor's head. I thought I saw the dark thing turn its head. I thought it was going to look at me, and I was suddenly frightened. I felt I didn't want to see its eyes –

'NO!' yelled Jef, making me jump. He'd dragged himself free of Mr Briggs' grip. 'I'm *not* going to leave. I have a right to be here. If this is a public amenity you can't throw me out. I'm an artist. If this is an arts centre I don't see why I have to leave, and you fat cats stay. What about OUR rights? What about me and my friends? We need this space, we found it –'

'*Darryl,*' snarled Mr Briggs, in a savage undertone, '*I'm warning you –*'

'We can *do* things with a raw place like this. Can't you see, this space isn't for a lady artist to do her dainty tapestry sewing or whatever it is. It's cold, it's draughty, it's nasty. We LIKE it that way. It's meant for us. You can't keep your Artist in Residence here. Take the old biddy somewhere else.'

The Press photographers were shoving each other out of the way to get a good look. The children were still oozing out of their corral. Everyone else was shifting about nervously, as if they were getting ready to flee the scene. Mr Briggs turned away from Jef in disgust, and beckoned to the burly workmen who were carrying in some smart new folding tables and chairs. They dumped the furniture and came through the crowd, bearing down on our gear. Big Dave stood there holding his chain and his toolbox, watching, stone-faced. (He told us later he was afraid that the police were going to be called.) Maddy had gone to Jef and was talking to him urgently, trying to get him to see reason.

Jef could be a pain but he wasn't totally crazy. If it had been anyone else telling him to leave he'd have behaved himself. It was just terribly unfortunate that Mr Briggs had to be the one who tried to throw him out. I saw Jef shake Maddy's hand off his arm, I saw his wild-eyed expression. I was scared he was going to swing a punch at one of the men, and our stuff was going to get smashed up.

'*I have been young*,' remarked the dumpy woman.

Everyone looked at her. She smiled at the Lord Mayor, Mr Briggs and the woman in apple-green. But it was Jef she was talking to. '*I have been young and I am now old, and I have never seen the righteous begging for bread …*'

At this, Big Dave suddenly grinned. Sister Dominic Mary, or Kathleen Dunne (because that's who it had to be) gave him a quick nod, as if acknowledging the only other rational person in the room. She could have been right. She turned to our art teacher. 'Mr Briggs,' she said, 'I don't think you have anything to worry about. I'm here to take part in the life of the arts in this community. If these young people are artists they can work alongside me. I'd be glad of the company, and I'm sure we'll learn from each other. It's a shame to waste all this grand empty space on one auld biddy.'

Jef blushed bright red. All the fight went out of him. You could almost see it go, like steam floating out of a kettle.

The Lord Mayor laughed.

'So,' remarked Dave, in the ensuing silence, speaking to the nun-artist. 'I won't need to change the locks then?'

'No,' said the Artist in Residence coolly. 'That won't be necessary.'

Mr Briggs scowled, but kept quiet.

'Well,' murmured the lady in apple-green, sounding bemused but deeply grateful that the row was over. 'Of course. Certainly … certainly.'

After that everything subsided, much to the disappointment of the Press, and the rest of the crowd too I expect. People always like catastrophes, as long as they're not going to get hurt themselves. Dave left. I didn't see him go. The Mayor made a shortish speech. The woman in apple-green was introduced by one of the lesser officials as 'Chloe Ridgemont-Brown, Director of the Bradfield Free Trade Gallery,' (our town's art gallery and museum). She made a longer speech, about re-visioning the wealth of our industrial past; the inestimable educational benefits of art; how grateful she was to Sister Kathleen for her patience over the delays and 'inevitable hitches'; and how splendid the new arts centre was going to be. The Artist in Residence made a speech that lasted two sentences, and everybody clapped.

Sister Kathleen – as it seemed you were supposed to call her – went off up the stone steps to the stage which was to be her 'studio area', with the Mayor and everyone following behind her. I saw her begin to unwrap one of the canvas lumps. The waitresses and workmen had been setting up tables and chairs while the speeches were going on. They'd now started on tea-urns and crockery. Maddy gave me a nudge. She'd already hooked Jef with one of her famous '*don't argue just do it*' stares. We went over and offered to help.

'I thought you were supposed to be keeping an eye on this place,' hissed Maddy furiously to Jef, as we carried trays of tidbits, and he wheeled the hostess trolley of warm vol-au-vents and sausage rolls.

'I *did*.' he whispered back, with guilty indignation. 'I

was here every day, well practically. All right, not that many. But I did check it out, a couple of times. I mean, at least once. I'm certain I did.'

'Sure. And Elvis is playing Wembley Stadium next month.'

He giggled. 'Is that so? I heard it was Jerry Garcia, Jim Morrison and Janis.'

Maddy hefted her tray threateningly, eyes flashing. Jef was sickeningly unreliable: and he had no shame. 'Do you want a smoked salmon pinwheel in your face, rock-nerd?'

'Break it up!' I warned them. We were so near the brink of hysteria, I wouldn't have been surprised if they'd actually started to food-fight, right there in front of the VIPs.

So instead of rehearsing we spent that Saturday morning offering plates of teeny sandwiches and pouring tea. It was a bizarre experience. We'd moved our gear out of the way, but it was lying in a corner half unpacked. The reception guests wandered around eating sandwiches, occasionally giving the sound-to-light units very peculiar looks. But there seemed to be an agreement among the grown-ups to behave as if nothing was wrong. They could gossip about what had really happened later. For now they treated us as if we were some nice young teenagers who'd kindly come along to help out, and chatted falsely about the 'potential' of the new arts centre. Mr Briggs stayed out of our way.

The class of seven year olds, who were here as a token proof of the educational benefits of the Residency, swarmed everywhere, taking rubbings from the different surfaces, gabbing with Sister Kathleen, copying the giant daisies. They were the only people behaving naturally, except maybe the nun-artist. They seemed perfectly happy.

We didn't know what was going to happen to us. We

managed to consult with each other while handing around the food, but we couldn't decide whether Sister Kathleen's offer was serious. Would she really let us share the place? *Could* she do that? We were sure the organisers, especially Mr Briggs and Ms Chloe Ridgemont-Brown (Ms Dangly-Earrings, Jef called her) wouldn't agree. Probably we'd be chucked out anyway, as soon as the Mayor and the Press were off the scene. I was worrying about how we were going to get our *Hajetu* gear away from here. Would it all fit into one taxi?

'What are we going to do now?' I hissed to Jef and Maddy, as we were helping the catering staff to clear up.

'I dunno,' Jef muttered back. 'Play it by ear.' They both spluttered into giggles, but I'd lost touch with the funny side of things. I was back in crawl-off-and-die mode. It was all right for them, coming to the Powerhouse wasn't their idea. The whole mess was my fault.

In the end everyone left. The children went with their teacher. Chloe Ridgemont-Brown departed with the Mayor. The Press gave up hope of having a fight break out and took off with their cameras and tape-recorders. Mr Briggs, to my great relief, left with a bunch of other people without having another go at Jef. At last there was no one. Just us and Sister Kathleen. She sat down at one of the cafe tables (they were dark green, metal, on tubular legs): and gave us a nod that invited us to join her.

'I'm sorry I called you an old biddy,' said Jef, blushing violently again. 'I shouldn't have done that. I lost my temper.'

'We could see that,' she grinned.

'Do you really mean that we can share this place with you?' demanded Maddy, getting to the point.

'I don't see why not.'

'But why? After we were so rude to you,' she protested (nobly taking a share of Jef's blame). 'We practically broke in here, and ruined your reception. It was awful.

I'm very sorry about all that, Sister Kathleen. But you see, we'd lost our rehearsal space, and we thought this building was derelict –'

'Look, Ms Dunne –,' began Jef, and he scowled, 'or Sister Dominic Mary, or whatever we're supposed to call you. We're sorry we mucked up your big moment, we're incredibly embarrassed, and now we'll go. Don't think you have to do us any favours. You owe us nothing.'

I noticed that her hands, which were lying quietly on the tabletop, were red like her cheeks, and rough and calloused, with very short nails. I wondered what kind of embroidery gave you callouses.

'My given name's Kathleen,' she said. 'I was Dominic Mary for so long, it's peculiar-sounding. But I answer to Kathleen now. Ye can call me Sister though. I'll know who you're talking to with that, more easily than the "Ms". But don't be embarrassed,' she added. 'I know how it is. When I first came out of our Community, and had to deal with things of this world, I was always making mistakes, real howlers. Ye can't help it when you're inexperienced. How else are you going to learn?'

At that moment I felt I loved Sister Kathleen. I wasn't a terminal idiot, I was *inexperienced*. I still felt terrible, but I thought I might be able to live again.

She laughed. She didn't look mad at all. She looked sharp as mustard. 'You didn't do me any harm. Why should I bear a grudge? Don't worry, I meant what I said. And I'll make sure it happens.'

She glanced around the big, cold empty hall bitterly. 'Actually, I said what I did because I agreed with you – Jef, is it? You're absolutely right. This is no place for an auld biddy, or any kind of biddy at all. They've been putting me off and putting me off, and now I see why. There's no room for my work in that gallery down town, and look at the state of this dump. It's half finished. There's no heating. There's no telephone ... Did you know,' she added grimly, 'there isn't even a *toilet* yet?'

We left, after arranging to come back the next day to discuss how the time-sharing would work. It seemed discreet to leave the rightful occupier in possession for a while. We met in the morning at the Wild Park gates. It was one of those bright January days that seems like spring, when you look for buds on the trees and flowers in the grass, but there were still chunks of rotten ice in the goldfish pool. Maddy and I had been having second thoughts. She'd rung me up in the evening to talk it over, and we'd both agreed it wasn't going to work out. The Artist In Residence didn't know what she'd let herself in for. She'd never asked what kind of art we did. We couldn't possibly expect a nun to share her space with techno-music rehearsals. We'd have to wait until Dave had a free slot, that was the most sensible idea. But Jef, when we'd met him, had gone completely the other way.

'I don't know what your problem is,' he told us. 'The old lady's cool. And where are we going to find another place like the Powerhouse? That hook, the stone-age paintings on those industrial tiles … It's *intense*.' He waved his arms. 'It's *meant*, it's synchronicity, and it's our chance to hook some resources out of the middle-class art establishment. I've just got to know how it feels to move on that vast industrial stage … If you ask me, the nun will soon fade. She's a very nice person, she'll easily get them to move her somewhere more comfortable: and the Powerhouse will be ours.'

There was no arguing with Jef when he had a good rant under way. By the time we reached the clearing, he'd almost convinced us that he was right. The Powerhouse *was* fascinating, you see. There was something about it that pulled us in, made us feel that we had to stake our claim. We found the doors open. The big hall looked even more different than it had done in the fuss and crowd of the official reception. But its strangeness survived, through the scrubbed surfaces and the new furniture. The sinister infant-school wall paintings were still scrawled around the walls, and the Frankenstein pulley still loomed in the shadowy height of the dome. But the first thing we noticed was something we'd all forgotten. The main attraction, that 'vast industrial stage' had been taken over. It was Sister Kathleen's studio.

Sister Kathleen was up there. She called us to join her. She'd taken off more of the swathings of canvas from those huge lumps that she'd been showing to the Mayor and the official crowd yesterday. She was standing beside one of them in her long overall: she stared at it, scratched her rough grey hair, walked around it and stared from another angle.

'Just a moment,' she said. 'I have to think about this fellow …'

The things were unwrapped, but I still couldn't make out what they were meant to be. From down below it had looked as if the stage was scattered with a collection of life-size fake standing-stones, like a fibreglass mock-up of Stonehenge. Close up they were more like burial mounds than stones. In between the two biggest stood a work table, already spread with a strangely varied litter of brushes, knives, coils of wire, paint-stained rags, tubs of glue, scraps of coloured fabric …

'I'll need to be on my own to work,' said Sister Kathleen, still frowning and walking round her lump. 'So will you three, I guess. You're musicians, I take it. Well, the sound system is soon going to be operational, they tell me; so that will be fine. Ye'll have to sit down with me and we'll work out a rota. You, me, my school groups and adult education workshops. And the floorlayers, and the heating engineers. It's going to be a proper jigsaw of activity in here, but we'll fit it all together. That's something you learn from living in a Community. I swear to God, I know more about accommodating other people and still getting my own work done, than if I was the Prime Minister.'

'How did you know we were musicians?' blurted Jef.

She glanced down into the hall. 'That's your set–up down there, isn't it. The synth, and the decks, and those peculiar doo-dahs that do the sound and light effects? What else would you be but musicians? Besides, your man Dave told me. He came round this morning to have a chat. He's left you the amps and speakers you'll see there. He says you're to hire them for the meanwhile, but not for much. He'd loan you them free, but then he wouldn't be covered on his insurance. He seems a good man to have on hand, your friend Dave.'

We three all looked at the burial mound that she was studying. There didn't seem to be any embroidery on it. It was hollow inside, something like a rough-cast Father Christmas grotto in a department store. A grotto for one child and Santa, no room for any elves or fairies. We were dying to ask what it was meant to be, but I think we were all too self-conscious. We'd taken no notice of the Artist in Residence blah-blah in school, on principle; and yesterday we'd learned nothing more. It seemed rude to show our ignorance, now that she was being so generous. I couldn't think of anything polite to say. It was a big fat lump. I couldn't see any art in it, any meaning at all. It was Jef, of course, who jumped in.

'Are you a sculptress then?'

She pulled a face. 'I'd be a sculptor if I was anything. No, not exactly. I wouldn't call myself that.'

'We thought you'd do embroidery, or weaving has- socks,' he explained, tactlessly. 'Something Holy.'

'I started off in watercolours,' she answered, continu- ing to study her burial mound. 'They never satisfied me. I wanted to make my pictures big, and all in the round. I didn't want people to stand outside. I wanted them to be *inside it*. I wanted to engage all the senses. And memory, especially memory. You know the way it is. Anything that comes into your head: a line of a poem, a scene from your childhood, brings so many other things along with it. I wanted to include them all. So I started building my *immersions*, that's what I call them. It's hard to find time or space for such big pieces of work in our Community, but Mother Superior said I had to do what felt right, or I was refusing my vocation. Then I had a little exhibition, and that's when I became a wee bit famous, who knows why.'

'Is that when you gave up being a nun?' demanded Jef.

She'd been talking without looking at us, almost to herself. She looked around then, surprised. 'Whatever gave you that idea? I haven't given up being a nun!'

'You said you'd left the Community, and gone back to using your real name.'

She blinked. 'Oh, that. I had to leave the Community House to organise my exhibition. It was a terrible experience. I'd never lived in the world since I was nineteen, and I'd never known how little I was missing. Gosh, I was glad to get home. And the name ... well, that's my stubborn nature. We're all to use our Baptismal names now: but I'm always going to be hankering after the old-fashioned ways, from when I first Entered.' She chuckled. 'You can't break the habit of a lifetime ... Though we only wear our habits for best, these days. I don't miss that. Not at all! I was never the type to look well in a robe and wimple.' She grinned, but then her face fell. 'The trouble is, I take up so much room. We don't live in a great vast barn of a place, not any more. And the cost of my materials is shocking. I'm trying to learn to think small. But when this Artist in Residence offer came along, it seemed like a gift from God.'

'I don't see how anyone with any self-respect can be a nun these days,' declared Jef. 'It's like joining the foreign legion, like a bank robber running off to South America. People do it to forget how inadequate they are in real life. If you want to help people, you could do that better without taking vows and shutting yourself away. Don't you feel like a hypocrite? Isn't being a nun just a way of escaping from reality, a soft way out? You said yourself, it's more comfortable in the convent ...'

The grotto was a framework covered with layers of different materials, some of it rough, some silky smooth; all in shades of translucent grey. I had started staring at it hard, because Jef was being so awful. I could see it wasn't finished. In places you could see the bare surface of some kind of moulded plastic. I looked at a bunch of electrical leads that trailed out from under the grey rigid skirts. They led to a black box that stood on the big table. I wondered what it was for.

Jef didn't mean to be nasty. He'd have thought it was dishonest and wrong to work beside Sister Kathleen without telling her his opinion of her life. He throws people who aren't used to his style, but if you get to know him you soon learn to brush it off ... though his idea of honesty doesn't go down too well with some teachers. I was surprised to see that Sister Kathleen was obviously upset by this attack. She'd seemed so tough and calm, but she winced as if he'd hit her.

'Maybe we're all inadequate sometimes,' she answered, her mouth twisting painfully. 'Maybe we all need to take shelter, at some point in our lives –'

'*I have desired to go,*' said Maddy, softly, '*Where springs not fail. To fields where flies no sharp and sided hail, and a few lilies blow ...*'

Sister Kathleen looked at her gratefully. 'Gerard Manley Hopkins.' She smiled, recovering her twinkle. 'Well, you may be right Jef. There was a little of that, of seeking a refuge from the cruel world, when I chose this life. *Where springs not fail.* I won't deny it. But it wasn't the whole story.'

Maddy always knew the right thing to say.

Jef, unabashed, jerked his head at the lump. 'Does it have a title?'

'It does. But you won't understand if you only see the outside.' She leaned over and flicked some switches on the black box. The grey surface came alive. Washes of colour, mostly blues and greens, spread and glimmered in the grey. She nodded to me encouragingly. 'Youngest first,' she said. 'That was the rule in my family. Try it and see.'

I walked in to the hollow place. I must have triggered a sensor in the floor or stepped through a beam, because at once I was surrounded by what seemed like the sound of the sea. A curtain of coloured light had dropped behind me and over me: a dancing mass of silver sparkles in a veil of steely-blue. I could see through it, but it was as Sister Kathleen had said. I was *immersed*. I looked to see what there was at the back of the cave, and found myself apparently gazing towards a far, blue horizon. The wide shadows of clouds passed over me, and the sharp-edged shadows of birds. Everything was moving. I knew I was standing on the stage in the Powerhouse, but it was exactly as if I was in a boat, sweeping up and down through the swell of the waves, over the cool glitter of the ocean. Then there were different colours: green, and splashes of scarlet; lilac and pink and indigo. I was going somewhere. I could see as if in my mind's eye the place where I was heading. It was a summer garden, full of the hum of insects. I heard a voice, speaking low, to a firm, marching beat. It said:

I will arise and go now, and go to Innisfree …
Nine beanrows will I have there, a hive for the honey-bee

This is lovely, I thought. What a lovely idea. But then it changed. The single voice became many voices, all speaking very low, until I was surrounded by a muttering crowd (I could tell that it was all the same voice, sampled and distorted, but that didn't weaken the effect). The marching beat had become grim. I could hear tramping

—— 42 ——

feet. On the inner wall of the cave, through the washes of beautiful colour, I began to see streets of buildings, men with rifles, crowds of people with angry and brutal, bitter faces – all in flickering, jerky black and white, like an old newsreel film. I heard gunfire; I think I saw someone being shot by a firing squad. Still the voices kept on, repeating the poem about peace in a summer garden; and the scarlet of the bean flowers fell like drops of blood.

The lights faded and the sound died. The glimmering water and the garden, the grey ghosts of a city's streets, all vanished. I was standing in a plastic cave, the ordinary light of a January afternoon coming through its dull walls. I stepped out, blinking and feeling dizzy.

'I call that one "Easter Rising," said Sister Kathleen, modestly. 'It's not finished yet.'

Jef tried the 'immersion' on the other side of the table, which was (she said) a seascape. The outside was gold and grey; studded with little shells, and patches of real sand stuck on with glue. It was called 'Immortality'. Maddy tried a third, which was even less finished than the other two, and was called 'My Heart Is Like A Singing Bird'. Sister Kathleen said that one was a 'love scene'. Somehow, she'd fixed it so that you could hear and see surprisingly little from the outside, so I didn't find out what the other two immersions were like. The grottos could be quite close to each other, without one person's experience leaking out and interfering with somebody in the next door scene.

I know I was impressed and I was sure the others were too. But it's hard to praise someone to their face. Besides, I think we felt she'd played a trick on us. She wasn't the kind of artist a nun had any right to be. *Embroidered vestments, tapestry hassocks, illuminated prayer books* … She wasn't anything like that. She was a techno-artist, like us. In a stupid way, I think, I was ashamed that I'd been moved by the nun-artist's work. I'd have preferred to be cynical, it would have been more dignified. We stood there, when we'd each had our 'immersions', in an awkward silence. I finally managed to say, 'It's a quotation from Yeats, isn't it? In my one.'

Sister Kathleen didn't seem to feel awkward. I suppose she was used to people not knowing what to say. 'Yes,' she agreed cheerfully. 'That's from a poem by W. B. Yeats. The other two nearly-complete works I've brought here, are based on poems by Christina Rossetti and by Wordsworth. That's usually how I get started. Sampling from the classics. I believe you modern rock-musicians do a lot of that yourselves.' She smiled, with just a little touch of mischief.

'I think your "love scene" is beautiful,' declared Maddy. 'It's like you said, it's what happens in your mind. Words and memories and colours and sounds, all together.'

Even Jef had the grace to mumble something. 'It's naive stuff, of course, and you've chosen hideously bland, obvious poems. But it's interesting.'

'Uh-huh,' she said doubtfully.

'That thing you said about "a terrible beauty is born",' I remembered. 'That was a quotation too.'

She laughed, and went redder in the face. 'Ye see, I'm not used to talking for no good reason. I'm used to silence. I put wee scraps of quotations in my work and I come out with quotes on all occasions, because it's the only words I can find in my mind. People must think I'm mad.'

'I know,' said Maddy. 'Why don't we leave you to finish your set-up, and we'll go and make a cup of tea in the kitchen. Then we can talk about this rota.'

Maddy and Jef went off down the stone stairs, which had been painted glossy dark green, with a smart new handrail to match. I lingered. Sister Kathleen had picked up a craft knife and was walking around 'Easter Rising' again, moving in now and then to scrape at the surface or cut something away. I watched her, and I had the feeling of *silence*. It's a feeling that comes over me sometimes when I'm practising well. Music can make a stillness round you when you know it by heart, when you are right inside it. I watched Sister Kathleen, Kathleen Dunne. I thought of hours of this silence, welling through a big house like invisible water. I saw figures in graceful robes gliding through quietness, with faces as calm and bright as hers was now. I wanted to ask her why did she have to spoil *The Lake Isle of Innisfree*, (which was one of my favourite poems) by bringing in all the grim marching and the angry crowds. I felt badly about that. It was as if she'd told me there was poison at the heart of anything beautiful.

I didn't ask my question. Just then, I noticed for the first time that Sister Kathleen had positioned her work-table right over the spot where my 'cold patch' had been. I had never said a word to Maddy or Jef about the strange experience I'd had in here, that snowy day when I found the Powerhouse. As I told you before, I'd forgotten, or blanked out of my mind, the utter horror that had overwhelmed me. I'd almost managed to convince myself that the version I'd told the little boys was true: I'd seen a rat, (my old friend the rat!), and that was what had scared me. But I remembered well enough what had really happened, when I was dancing and singing up here, to stop me from wanting to talk about it. I'd almost warned them, that other afternoon in Dave's office: but I'd been glad afterwards that I'd kept my mouth shut. I especially didn't want Jef to know. I did not want him to start investigating my 'paranormal experience'. I suppose it was childish, but I just wanted to leave well alone.

I looked at the worktable, and realised that the three times we'd come back to the Powerhouse, I'd always been able to *feel* that spot up on the stage. I could have led you to it blindfold, though I'd have hated to have to do it. I felt a rush of pure relief, because Sister Kathleen, by accident or on purpose, had made it impossible for anyone to do what I had done. That was when I finally, consciously, decided I was never going to tell Maddy or Jef. I would protect them from their own curiosity. There was nothing spooky about the rest of the Powerhouse. We'd be quite safe.

'Do you believe in ghosts?' I demanded, suddenly.

She looked at me with such a sharp, intelligent glance that I *knew* she knew exactly why I'd asked this odd question. 'No,' she said. 'I do not.'

'Oh.'

I thought it was a peculiar thing for a nun to say. Surely nuns of all people were supposed to believe in the supernatural. But I didn't want to talk to Sister Kathleen either about the experience I'd had up here. So I left it at that.

Three

*A*FTER AN AWESOMELY BAD START, THE POWERHOUSE turned out to be a brilliant piece of good luck for *Hajetu*. The building and decoration firms, having ruined the official opening, suddenly got themselves organised. Within a fortnight new flooring was down, central heating was installed, the sound system was wired up, and we had a toilet. We even had a brand new shiny kitchen where we could make coffee and eat biscuits. We had to give up the idea of rehearsing on the great big stage, because that was definitely Sister Kathleen's studio. But since the coffee bar and exhibition part of the centre wasn't opening until the summer, we had the lower hall to ourselves. Better than that, some tall honeycomb screens arrived. We could move them around to change the shape of the space, and it made a wonderful difference to the acoustics and the atmosphere. And this was all free, except for our share of the utility bills. We could rehearse every evening of the week, if we felt like it, unless Sister Kathleen had a workshop; and Saturday and Sunday too. We were going to be allowed to use the Powerhouse on this basis until Sister Kathleen's residency was over at the end of June: which was so far ahead, none of us even thought about it.

My brother Jerry was sick as an aviary full of parrots. He and Tom and Nicky had been with me the day we found the Powerhouse. As far as the boys were concerned I had treacherously betrayed them. I had handed over a great, spooky playground to the grown-ups, and let them 'ruin' it, just for the sake of my stupid techno group. They despised *Hajetu*. Their idea of musical excellence was a hit single from the latest children's TV cartoon characters; or a Premier League football squad. I took them along to see the new arts centre, and introduced them to Sister Kathleen. They were slightly mollified after that. Tom and Jerry decided it wasn't my fault. The Powerhouse had been doomed to be 'ruined' before I got involved. They no longer wanted any part of it. But they were hoping to negotiate with Sister Kathleen over one of those 'great big plastic rubbish boxes' of hers.

'One of them would make a terrific den,' Jerry told me. 'We could put it up at the bottom of our garden. Tell her we'll dump all the rubbish for her. We'll put it in the recycle.'

I said I'd let him know.

Best of all, maybe, Ms Chloe Ridgemont-Brown had noticed us. She decided that having some teenage techno-musicians involved in her arts centre was a really good idea. A few weeks after we'd moved in, just before half term, Dave Ramsey got us another gig. It was a real gig this time, no question of us being 'allowed' to play at being rock stars by Dave's friends. And we were playing support for another techno set-up, so we had an audience who would understand. We were terrified. Before we went on, Maddy and I barricaded ourselves into the Ladies' loo to finish our make-up. Maddy actually threw up, she was so scared. But she was okay. She came out of the toilet smiling bravely, looked into the mirror and said being sick certainly gives you a classy, ethereal pallor. She was wearing the Hipster Belt, over her glittery mock-snakeskin trousers, a snakeskin halter top and a gauze blouse. I fixed the tiny Paintbox Pickups onto her cheekbones. When she sang she'd have a rainbow musical aura swirling around her head. I was wearing a white shirt, black trousers and a fancy waistcoat, with my hair slicked back and spiked. Maddy's mother had done me a 'White Face' makeup, like they do in Chinese Opera. It had seemed like a good idea at the time, but now I peered into the mirror and thought the only good thing was that nobody could possibly recognise me.

'You look *intense*,' Maddy told me loyally. It was Jef's favourite word.

'I look like a snooker star who's collided with a fortune cookie.'

It wasn't all that funny, but we both collapsed in giggles …

We were good. The stage was well set up, the audience was full of people who knew what we were trying to do. Plus Jef's Mum, Maddy's Dad: plus my Mum and Dad lurking in the background. They'd rather I'd been playing Schubert or something, but at least they'd turned up. Apart from the cigarette smoke, which was dire, and the fact that I wasn't allowed to go into the 'bar area', because I wasn't fourteen, not a single thing went wrong for me, and Maddy and Jef seemed to be riding the same perfect wave. Jef flashed out the rhythms on his stomping Platform Souls, Maddy soared away with the melodies. At one point I saw, to my amazement, our patroness the Art Gallery Director standing in a corner. She was whispering something to the man next to her, and they were nodding.

'See that?' muttered Jef, taking a step back between numbers, to visit me where I was perched in the midst of my machines. 'That guy with old Dangly Earrings? That's Andrew Shine, the Festival Director.'

I nearly fell off my stool. Next thing we knew, we'd been invited to perform at the 'Festival Young Idea Finale', in the 'Marquee In the Park' in June. Mr Shine explained that we had to make a decision quickly, as the

Festival publicity was just about to go to press. He was afraid there wasn't time to get our pictures in the brochure, but having seen us in action he felt we couldn't be left out. It didn't take us long to make up our minds.

The only bad thing about this success was that it made us ungrateful to Sister Kathleen. We forgot how much we owed to her generosity. Jef started to get delusions of grandeur, and said he didn't want to be in the 'Marquee In The Park'. He wanted to throw out Sister Kathleen's exhibition, and have the 'Festival Young Idea Finale' in the Powerhouse. He said it was *obviously* a performance space, not an arts-and-crafts studio, and the Gallery Director and Andrew Shine ought to realise this. It was all Maddy could do to stop him from invading the Festival Office and explaining this dazzling idea to the people involved.

We were ungrateful to Dave Ramsey too. He soon came up with a slot at the Heavy Heart. He was very keen for us to take it up and leave the Powerhouse to Sister Kathleen. Naturally we refused: and I'm afraid we hurt his feelings.

Jef grumbled about having to keep out of the Powerhouse for Sister Kathleen's workshops; and even about sharing the kitchen. Maddy told Jef he was being a sexist pig, and the *real* reason he resented Sister Kathleen was because he thought a woman had no right to be doing big heavy-duty techno art. Jef sneered and jeered, and asked her when she was going to take the veil …

When I write all this down, I see there was more than one bad thing. I see that perhaps working in the Powerhouse was bad for us, in a way, right from the start. But that's hindsight. We didn't feel that anything was wrong, not at first. We didn't feel oppressed or uneasy, not consciously anyway. We felt we'd been incredibly lucky.

I did see my friend the rat again from time to time, in

those dark evenings at the end of winter. I'd see it creeping on the ledge where the light-sconces were fitted along the wall, or down on the floor boldly peeping out from behind one of the amps. It spooked me a little that nobody else seemed to notice our visitor. But I didn't mention it. If there *were* still rats about, in spite of all the cleaning and painting, they'd surely soon give up and go away. I certainly didn't think of it as part of a haunting. If anything, I was afraid there might be something up with *me*. I wasn't sleeping well. Perhaps I was seeing things, from working too hard.

It was Mrs Cosso, my piano teacher, who finally told me the story, the secret history of the place I called the Powerhouse. Mrs Cosso had been a concert pianist before she retired, and she had a very good reputation as a teacher. She was old, and fat, and she liked to wear low-cut lacy blouses that showed acres of smooth pale skin, soft and thick like whipped ice-cream. She had tiny feet, on which she wore little flat satin slippers with diamante embroidery. They looked far too small to carry her. I was always amazed when I saw her get up and walk, even across the room. She lived in a first floor flat in one of the big Victorian houses opposite the Wild Park, and I don't think she ever went out. All day, when she wasn't teaching, she did nothing but sit: watching the world through her lace-curtained windows. She had a lady-who-does, who did her shopping and cleaning, and friends who came to play bridge. She had arthritis, a voice like a foghorn, and she told immense whoppers about her fabulous career and her handsome, dashing husbands. She'd had three, all of them rich and glamorous. I loved Mrs Cosso, because unlike my Mum and Dad she knew when to stop. Sometimes I'd come along to a lesson, and after about five minutes she'd say 'Well, this isn't doing any good,': get out the cards and teach me to play bridge instead.

One day, when I'd been playing really badly and we'd stopped early for a bridge lesson, Mrs Cosso casually said. 'It's not surprising that the Artist in Residence gets away as often as she can. I hear she's off to Birmingham again this weekend.'

Sister Kathleen's Community House (she never called it a convent, so we didn't either) was in Birmingham. It was too far to commute, so while she was Artist in Residence she was living with some other nuns, who had a flat on the rundown estate beside the park. They weren't the same brand of nuns, but apparently that didn't matter. They were Notre Dames and Sister Kathleen was a Sacred Heart, I learned later: but I was never very clear about the difference. Mrs Cosso and her friends didn't approve of these other nuns, who ran something called a Drop-In Centre. They all hated the tower block estate, because it was too near the big old houses where *they* had their flats, and it made them feel that they lived in the poor part of town. They said nuns should not have moved into such a disreputable area. Nuns were supposed to help the disadvantaged, but they ought not to mix with the 'wrong sort of people'.

'Oh really?' I murmured.

'No, it's not surprising at all. *Some* people I know are shocked that a nun would want to be associated with a place with such an evil reputation. Not that I think the same, but you know what some people are like … I suppose you know the dreadful old story.'

'I don't know any stories about the Powerhouse,' I answered, looking at my cards. 'It was simply a disused industrial building, far as I'm aware.'

Mrs Cosso drew in her breath between her teeth, with a soft hiss. 'So you don't know about the murders?' I shook my head. I saw from the way her eyes lit up that she'd been dying to tell me about these murders, ever since I told her about *Hajetu* moving into the Power-house, but her conscience had stopped her.

Mrs Cosso rather approved of *Hajetu*. She hated the thought of being labelled a fuddy-duddy, and she also thought it was good for me. *Have something about you that the media people can latch on to,* she used to say. *Doesn't matter how well you play the piano, that's not something they can understand. Have glamorous husbands, have affairs, dress divinely … Then you'll have them on your side.* A sideline in sound-to-light unit music was not as good as marrying a jet-setter, she implied, but it was better than nothing.

'I really shouldn't,' she murmured. 'It's not a very nice story.'

'But you did say it was a long time ago.'

'Oh, it was. Must be nearly twenty-five years ago now.' She hissed again, shaking her head: and I kept quiet. She loved to tell me awful things, but if I seemed too interested she'd sometimes get an attack of propriety, and shut up. 'Well,' she sighed. 'If you must know … in fact there were three murders. Three young girls. The first girl was one of those hippies, as young people called themselves then. Flower power, pop music: just your sort of thing, my dear. She died at a concert they called a "Happening", that was held in the derelict pumping station, back in 1972 I think. I'm not sure of the date, but she cut her own throat, right up there on the stage. The poor child.'

I was riveted. 'I thought you said it was murder. How come she cut her own throat?'

'Ah. That was what they thought at first! There were three artistes. I can't recall their real names at the moment, but the girl's stage name was Sunshine. Her death was supposed to be an accident – though goodness knows how anyone could cut their own throat by accident. Well, it all blew over. The building was boarded up, the case was closed. Then not long after, another girl was found lying in a pool of blood, in the very flat where one of the two brothers was living. There were two brothers you see, who were in the band with Sunshine. She – the second victim – was supposed to have killed herself. But when the *third* girl was found, that was when it all came out. The brothers had tried to bury the body that time. But someone found her, and the police connected her with the young men – there was blood all over one young man's car, and, oh, the evidence against them was so clear that the older brother, I think it was, confessed. Confessed to all three murders, and was put away for a long time. Not the younger one, he got off. It was such a scandal because all the young people of the town had been going to those hippie parties in the old pumping station. Dabbling in drugs and I don't know what, and we grown-ups were supposed to be fuddy-duddies if we objected. But then we saw what it could all lead to …'

Mrs Cosso stopped talking abruptly. I think I'd been keeping too quiet. She narrowed her eyes at me suspiciously. 'It was a very long time ago,' she repeated. 'I wouldn't have mentioned it, only I thought you *must* have heard something, since you're working there. But it's nothing for you to worry about, my dear. Water under the bridge, all forgotten and forgiven. Now what are you going to bid, with those cards, in reply to three hearts?'

I was very shocked. No one had ever said anything to us, or to Sister Kathleen as far as I knew, about the Powerhouse having been the scene of a murder. I could hardly believe the story was true. Mrs Cosso *did* sometimes get carried away. But I realised, sitting there in my cosy armchair beside the big, glowing, rosewood baby grand, and shivering with astonishment, that this story might explain my cold spot. Someone had been murdered, up there on the Powerhouse stage …

I didn't tell Maddy and Jef. I'd decided not to tell them

about the cold spot, and this was part of the same thing. I knew they'd be thrilled to know they were working in a haunted arts centre. But I was scared. Leave well enough alone, I kept thinking, and it can't hurt you. I'm not sure what I meant by 'it', but that was what kept running through my mind. Leave well enough alone. What I didn't know, was that Maddy had also been getting interested in the Powerhouse's past: and fate (or something) was about to take a hand.

A few weeks after half term the weather, which had been damp and mild, turned icy. The newly-installed central heating system had never worked properly. Ms Ridgemont-Brown had been trying to get it improved, but the workmen's burst of activity was over. Extra radiators and more lengths of copper pipe had arrived, but nothing else had happened. We'd been using electric fires that we'd borrowed from our families; and there was a huge, rattling old convector heater up on the stage. It was still chilly in there, especially after dark. One evening I arrived and found Jef and Maddy already in the hall, but they hadn't started setting up. Maddy said she thought she'd pulled a muscle, and she didn't want to exercise in the cold. Then Jef said he had a sore throat.

I was feeling tired and lack-lustre myself. I'd just had my birthday. Mum had taken me and Jerry and Solange out to my favourite Tex Mex restaurant. It was a shame Dad couldn't make it, but you can't have everything. It had been a good evening, on the whole. I'd told Mum I didn't want a party, and she'd accepted that. But she couldn't understand why I hadn't invited Maddy and Jef. I'd tried to tell her that they were *sixteen*, and they were *colleagues*, not exactly friends. I hadn't asked them because I was sure they'd have better things to do. Better not to ask than to be turned down.

'It's always so filthily cold in here,' complained Jef.

I knew where the cold came from. It seeped from that

place up on the stage, that column of dead and icy air. But I couldn't tell him that. I thought Maddy and Jef were looking at each other, trying to signal that they wished I was out of the way. That was what the 'pulled muscle' and the 'sore throat' meant …

'Okay,' I said. 'If we're not going to rehearse, I suppose I might as well go home.'

'No,' said Maddy. 'Don't go. Let's make ourselves some coffee. Let's huddle round the fire and talk. Have you ever wondered, you two, about the history of this place?'

'It was a water–pumping station,' I offered, uneasily.

She shook her head. 'I know that. I've seen Ms Ridgemont-Brown's leaflets. No, I meant … there must be more information. But how can we find out? I bet if we could get into that room under the stage, we'd discover some secrets. Wait a minute, I'll put the kettle on.'

To get to the kitchen she had to walk by the door under the stage, the door that had always been locked. It had been cleaned and repainted along with the rest of the place, but none of us had ever seen what lay beyond. One of Jef's major grumbles against Sister Kathleen was that she had a complete set of keys. We only had a latchkey. If we ever wanted to get into the building apart from prearranged times, if Sister Kathleen wasn't here someone had to trek over and fetch the caretaker, who lived in the same estate where the nuns had their Drop-In Centre. But his set did not include a key to the undercroft.

'I bet it's nothing but a damp hole full of rubble,' I said.

Maddy laughed. But she rattled the doorhandle as she passed, anyway, and gave it a mild shove. To our complete amazement, the door slowly began to open inward. It shifted about ten centimetres. Then it stopped.

'Hey!' exclaimed Jef. 'It's our lucky night!'

'Stop!' I cried. 'We're not supposed to go in there. You know we're not!'

'Why not?' demanded Jef. 'Why shouldn't we? The door's open. Don't you want to know what's inside? Don't you want to know where the bodies are buried?'

'There won't be any bodies!'

Maddy and Jef looked at me strangely. Maddy bit her lip. 'Come on Robs,' she coaxed. 'What's wrong? Of course there won't be any bodies. Don't you want to explore?'

Suddenly I was sure I wasn't the only one who was hiding something. But I gave in.

'All right,' I said, trying to laugh. 'But don't blame me if we get into trouble.'

She pushed the door again. It moved reluctantly, opening on to a dark, dark space.

'I'll fetch a torch!' offered Jef. He hurried away, and returned in a moment with the big utility flashlight that was kept in the caretaker's stores. The beam was strong. It played over strange shapes that lay inside there; raising glints of colour and glitters of reflection. I couldn't make anything out clearly. It was like peering into a tomb, disturbing thousands of years of dust and mystery ... Our eyes started to get accustomed to the gloom, as the light from the brightly-lit hall behind us dispersed the darkness. A room emerged around the torch beam: a long, low room. It was not the rubbish dump I'd predicted. Everything was blurred by dust, as if we were peering through murky water. But it seemed to be furnished and decorated. Maddy found a lightswitch. She tried it. Nothing happened. She turned the beam upwards. We saw cobwebby red and gold Christmas decorations festooned from corner to corner of the low ceiling, and an empty socket dangling on a cord.

'Spare lightbulb!' cried Jef, and rushed away again.

When he came back, Jef and Maddy took the plunge

and groped their way in. I stayed by the door. Jef clambered on to what seemed to be a low table, and tried the bulb he'd brought. Luckily it fitted the old fashioned socket, because we had to have bulbs that would fit the old sconces along the walls of the lower hall.

'Try the switch again,' they called to me.

I switched on the light.

'Wow!' breathed Jef. 'Aladdin's Cave!'

'My God!' exclaimed Maddy.

'*Eygptian tomb*,' I whispered.

It was all there, the stuff that I'd forgotten. The carousel horse, the purple curtains, the papier-mâché tree. It looked as if the workmen, when they cleared out the lower hall, had simply opened the door to the undercroft, shoved all the litter in here, and locked it again. But there was more. Painted stage flats, giant artificial flowers, an acoustic guitar with broken strings, a huge basket overflowing with fancy dress clothes. There was a long wicker sofa and two chairs to match, the kind with high, round backs called 'peacocks' tails'; a squashy pouffe sewn of patchwork leather; a makeshift bookcase built of bricks and planks. All the furniture was draped in fabric, with patches of vivid patterns and colour showing through the grime. The low table that Jef had been standing on was swathed in paisley velvet. The walls were hung with more fabric, and plastered with dusty posters.

'Amazing!' shouted Jef, peering into the basket. He pulled out a pair of thigh-length patent leather boots. '*Look* at this stuff!'

'Incredible!' exclaimed Maddy, lifting up a poster that had slipped to the floor, and shaking showers of dust from the face of the fallen idol. It was Jimi Hendrix. 'I bet these are worth money – or would be, if they were in better nick. Vintage about 1968.'

'Flower power,' declaimed Jef, draping a broken

feather boa around his neck and dancing around. He picked up a lump the size of a cannonball from the table, and blew off the muck to reveal a purple candle in the shape of a skull, decorated with crimson flames. 'Hippies, happenings, far-out, man!'

Maddy had found a chimney-shaped old paraffin fire that had been used as a cooking stove, still crusted with ancient food stains; and a fruit crate full of plates and mugs and pans, 'People have been living here!' she announced. 'Look at it. There were people living here, camping out in secret splendour, maybe twenty or thirty years ago. And then one day they walked out, leaving everything behind. The door was locked, and nobody's been in here since. How weird! I wonder why. Why did they leave so suddenly?'

I stood in the doorway, watching.

'What's wrong, Robs?' asked Maddy, suddenly noticing I hadn't moved.

'Rats,' I said. It was a good excuse, it might be true. My friend the rat had to live somewhere.

'Ugh! Did you see one?'

'Well, no. But it looks likely.'

'Great,' declared Jef. 'I know a man with a terrier. We'll have a rat hunt.'

'We will not!' shrieked Maddy. 'Leave the rats alone!'

She threw a cushion at him. Jef threw one back. I could hardly see them for dust, but I could hear them coughing, whooping and laughing in excitement.

They were right. It was a fantastic find, a fabulous time capsule. It was so strange to know that this incredible den had been here all along, while we were rehearsing our futuristic music outside. It had been here when the workmen were fitting floors and laying cable. It had been here when I explored a mysterious derelict shell of a building, that day in the snow. But I was thinking, sometimes there's a curse on whoever disturbs the tomb.

But none of us fell ill, or died in mysterious circum-
stances. Instead, we began to clean up the undercroft.
Every rehearsal evening we found the door still unlocked,
and instead of practising we moved in there with supplies
borrowed from the cleaners' closet. Jef decided that the
door had probably never been locked at all. We'd never
asked about it, we'd simply grumbled privately about not
having the key. It must have swollen shut, so that nobody
could get in. The wood had dried out and shrunk again,
since the Powerhouse had been refurbished and the
central heating had kicked in (sort of!) and that explained
the mystery.

We shook out the hangings and swept the floor. We
got rid of most of the dust, and then started in with mops
and buckets of hot water. We discovered heaps of weird
hippie regalia: home-made scented candles, strange
screen prints, a tattered tarot pack thrust down behind
the cushions on the wicker sofa; some ugly little curios
arranged on a bookcase; some falling-apart paperback
science fiction novels; a canvas sack full of what seemed
to be motor bike parts. The table Jef had been standing
on turned out to be a surprisingly elegant coffee table,
with some very weird pictures sandwiched inside the
thick glass top. I got over my fear. It's hard to feel
haunted when you are doing housework, in a room that
smells of floor-cleaner. I felt sorry for the people whose
things we were turning over. It seemed so pitiful that they
should be gone, and these helpless objects left to lie here
all through the years, waiting for someone to come back.

Maddy and Jef talked a lot about the mystery. Who
had left these relics behind? Were they the same people
who had painted the flowers on the tiles in the hall? Why
had the door been locked, or if it hadn't been locked why
had nobody forced it open before now? Why hadn't this
nice dry basement been cleared out, and put to some use
in the new art centre ... ? I could have told them Mrs

Cosso's story. But I didn't. If they knew about the murder story, I felt certain they'd get onto the idea that the Powerhouse was haunted. I knew I couldn't cope with that. And yet I'd have to cope, because Maddy and Jef wouldn't understand if I said I was scared.

I was so afraid of being left out, you see. That was what it always came back to.

A week after we opened the 'tomb', the curse fell on us. I arrived at the Powerhouse first for once, and I quickly began to set up for a rehearsal. When Maddy and Jef turned up, I said that I thought we ought to do some work for a change. Maddy pleaded – with a sly smile – that she'd like to have a few minutes in the undercroft first. I was startled by that smile. It didn't look right on Maddy: Maddy was never sly. Maybe Jef felt the same.

'You're getting addicted,' he accused her. 'What d'you mean "a few minutes"? You know once you get in there, we'll never be able to drag you out.'

Maddy laughed. 'You could be right,' But then she looked quite serious, and more like Maddy. 'I just feel … there's something important in there. Something we have to find out.' She went to the door, took hold of the handle and pushed. Nothing happened. She rattled the handle again. 'Let me,' said Jef. They both tried shoving hard: it was no good.

The door was locked.

Then somebody coughed. We all three jumped and spun around guiltily. We saw the last two people we'd expected: Mrs Ogden and Mrs Turner, the Powerhouse cleaners. We'd hardly met these two women. They were never at work when we were around. Sometimes they left us notes, when we hadn't done the washing up; or we'd left what they considered 'a mess'. That was usually our only contact with them. Mrs Ogden, the small fat one who was always scowling, was holding up something in her hand.

'Are you looking for this?' she asked triumphantly.

It was a key. It must, obviously, be the key to the door under the stage.

'You're not to go in there,' said Mrs Turner sternly. She was the tall one with the droopy lower lip, who smoked a lot. 'Ms Ridgemont-Brown said that door was to stay locked, and Sister Kathleen said we were never to let you have the key.'

'I don't know how it came about that it was left open,' broke in Mrs Ogden. 'But it won't happen again. You're to stay out of there.'

'But why?' protested Maddy. 'We weren't doing any harm!'

'I don't know what you were doing and I don't care,' stated Mrs Ogden majestically. 'I'm going by what Sister Kathleen told me. Now, if you're going to practise your music, you can stay. Otherwise, you'd better go home. We're going to have to clean this floor, you left such a mess last night, treading dirt from that basement.'

We packed away our gear and left. Jef started to cackle the moment we were outside. 'I've never been so insulted in all my life!' he squawked.

But Maddy was solemn. 'I was afraid that was going to happen,' she said gravely. 'We're on to something, that's their problem. Look, I don't want to talk here. Or in school. We'll have to meet somewhere else. I'll fix it up. I've found out something really incredible.'

Four

MADDY CALLED A MEETING IN THE REFERENCE Library in town. We went there together after school, still in our uniforms. She led us up to the Rotunda, which had once been the main Reading Room, but was now a graveyard for extinct forms of data storage: microfiche viewers, stacks and stacks of tatty local and national newspapers; massive rows of out of date encyclopedias and yearbooks. It was quiet in there, very quiet. Maddy sat down at one of the empty tables, and took out a fat card folder from her school briefcase.

We were alone except for the librarian at her desk and one old lady with a green eyeshade, who was surrounded by masses of tomes about International Shipping, and completely lost in her research.

'I've been wondering about the Powerhouse,' said Maddy quietly. 'Since, well, I'm not sure. It could be since the day we moved in. I thought there was something wrong. The way the building work didn't get done, and Ms Ridgemont-Brown didn't seem to know what was going on. It was good fun, when they all turned up for the grand opening and nothing was ready ... but it was pretty strange. Didn't you think so?'

Jef shrugged. 'I assumed it was natural. Builders are like that. Famous for it.'

'Well, maybe. But there was Dave Ramsey too. I didn't think of it at the time, but later I was sure he knew something. That afternoon when we went to him after the shed was knocked down, and Robs described the Powerhouse. He knew something that he wasn't telling us.'

She opened the folder. I could see that it was full of photocopied newsprint, and a stack of other papers. That's one thing I forgot to tell you about Maddy. She was an incredibly thorough person. She did all her school work as if she was preparing for the Nobel Prize. 'So ... I didn't say anything to you two, basically because I thought I couldn't tell Robs without telling you, Jef: and you're such a blabbermouth.'

'True,' agreed Jef, humbly.

'But I decided to work on Dave. I went and offered to help him with his filing. He didn't suspect a thing. Dave's so busy running that whole business on his own, he has to let everything but the immediate problems slide. He was pitifully grateful. I've been working in the Heavy Heart, Sunday mornings. Dave never throws anything away. I soon found what I was searching for. Look at these.'

She showed us a sheaf of letters and leaflets. Most of the letters were official – printed circulars from the Town Hall or the Free Trade Gallery or the local Arts Council. 'He gets all this stuff because he had a grant to start up the Heavy Heart. That makes him what they call an "Arts Entrepreneur", and he's on their mailing lists. Read these. They're in date order, you'll be able to follow the plot.'

Jef and I took a handful each, and stared at them blankly.

Maddy sighed. 'Oh, all right. I'll explain. It goes like this. Years ago, the Gallery and the City Council acquired a parcel of land beyond the Wild Park, including some derelict waterboard buildings. But they never did anything, except make vague plans to knock the buildings down. When Chloe Ridgemont-Brown was appointed Director she found some plans for a new Arts Centre to be built on that land, and asked why nothing had been done. Everyone told her that the scheme was far too expensive. So she decided the old pumping station – that's the Powerhouse – could be converted; and that would be much cheaper. She's keen on recycling old industrial buildings. She goes on about it in all her letters and things. No one could think of a good excuse why not, so the redevelopment began. But the work didn't get done. No local builders would touch the contract. Different firms came and went. Ms Ridgemont-Brown's not from around here. She had no idea why everything was crashing as soon as it left the ground, because there was one vital piece of information she didn't know. The building we call the Powerhouse was the scene of the first of a series of very mysterious murders, twenty-five years ago –'

I felt myself beginning to blush.

'– and no one told her anything,' finished Maddy, 'because for some reason, they couldn't bring themselves to tell the truth.'

'You mean, the builders wouldn't work on the Power-house because they were afraid of ghosts?' exclaimed Jef, green eyes widening in appreciation of a good story. 'Cool!'

I stared at a circular letter from Ms Ridgemont-Brown. 'Our plans are very far advanced. We have already invited Sister Kathleen Dunne to be our first Artist in Residence. Her work is such an exciting blend of the old and the new, of modern manufacturing technology and artistic power combined. I see The Source as a perfect showcase for her.' 'The Source' was the official name for the Powerhouse.

'Maybe,' said Maddy, slowly. 'But it's not funny Jef. There's something *wrong*. I feel sorry for poor Ms Ridgemont-Brown. She must have been truly sick when she found the ... the skeleton in the closet. But there was nothing she could do by then, except lock up the hippie den in the basement, and hope the newspapers didn't get on to the art centre's evil past.'

'But what's the problem?' demanded Jef. 'I don't see it. I mean, taking it for granted we none of us seriously believe in ghosts. People have got to be murdered *somewhere!* Probably hundreds of people have been murdered on the site of this library, since the dawn of human history: and who cares? What's the difference?'

His voice had risen to a semi-shout. There was a sharp clack-clack of high heeled shoes on the parquet floor. The librarian was suddenly beside us, glowering. 'If you can't keep quiet,' she whispered. 'You will have to leave. You're disturbing the other readers.'

'*What* other readers?' asked Jef sarcastically. He half stood up and gazed about dramatically. 'I'm looking round, and I can't *see* these "other readers" –'

The old lady with the green eyeshade didn't raise her head.

'That's enough! You'll have to leave!' snapped the librarian.

Jef could have apologised, but for some reason he'd flipped into his tantrum mode, and he wasn't going to back down: so we beat a retreat.

When we were safely outside the building we all burst into giggles. I don't know why. The gardens around the Library were dotted with Springtime crocuses and daffodils. Next door, beyond the stumps of grey wall that were all that remained of Bradfield's mediaeval castle, the Art Gallery raised its massive imitation-Greek columns. I imagined Ms Ridgemont-Brown spying on us from her office window.

'Wow!' hooted Jef. 'Quick, where's the nearest phone. We have a scandal to sell. Shall we go straight to the tabloids, or get ourselves a razor-sharp agent first?'

'We don't know what the scandal *is*, yet,' said Maddy mysteriously. 'But there's more about those murders. Let's find somewhere else where we can talk.'

We ran down the hill into the town centre, laughing. Directly below Castle Hill, where the Gallery and Library stand, is the posh-shopping part of Bradfield, which Jef hated like poison. He wouldn't normally have set foot in the dinky sandwich bar we hit on. It was lit too brightly, decorated like a sickly nursery and had tables made for Muppets. But at least it was open, and we could have a Muppet-table to ourselves.

He had calmed down by the time we settled with our cappuccinos. 'We've got to tell her,' he declared seriously. 'We have to tell Sister Kathleen. It's not that it's important. As I said, I don't see how it makes any difference to the Powerhouse being an arts centre. But it's the principle. It's disgusting that they didn't tell her.'

'Don't be stupid,' said Maddy to Jef (as if this was perfectly obvious). 'She knows. She's known all along. Dave Ramsey told her.'

Jef was silenced, briefly. I saw from his eyes he was staggered at how much Maddy knew. I felt the same. It was like: you've seen a vague shape in the water, felt scared and wondered if you were just being a cissy. Then the person who was swimming next to you says *that was a shark*, and tells you what kind, how big, how many teeth …

'But what is the whole story?' I demanded, shakily. 'What is there to tell? Some murders that we don't really know anything about, and a hippie den, that for some reason has to stay locked up. We don't even know if Sunshine –'

Maddy stared at me.

'How did you know her name!'

I started blushing so hard I thought my face would burst. 'Mrs Cosso told me,' I croaked. 'I didn't say

— 67 —

anything, because ... because ... didn't think you'd be interested ...'

Jef looked from one of us to the other. 'Seems like everybody's been keeping secrets,' he remarked.

'Yes,' said Maddy softly. 'I know the feeling, Robs. I didn't want to talk about this, either. I've been finding things out, and wondering what to do, whether I should keep quiet about it or if I should tell ... '

I couldn't meet her eyes.

Maddy pulled her briefcase up on to the table, and took out the fat folder again.

'Luckily,' she said, 'I've already copied everything I could find from the Rotunda files. About the murders, I mean. So we don't have to worry about Jef getting us banned.'

'I did not get us banned! I merely asked the woman, politely –'

Maddy ignored him. 'What did Mrs Cosso tell you, Robs?'

I swallowed hard. How I hated this whole business. 'Well, not much. Only that three girls were murdered, and the first one called herself Sunshine. And in the end someone confessed and went to prison. What else is there to know?'

So then Maddy told us the story of that long-ago tragedy, as she had pieced it together from the stored secret history in the Rotunda, and from Dave Ramsey's back pages. Jef kept interrupting, I stayed quiet.

'It began in 1970,' said Maddy. 'There was a local rock group, two boys and a girl. They were called *Steve, Mike and Sunshine*. Steve and Mike were brothers, Sunshine was really called Sophie. She was younger than the others, still at school when she met them. It was Steve and Mike who started to use the pumping station as a den. It was already derelict. They used to have wild parties in the undercroft, and they put on free concerts using the hall and the stage, the way we've imagined doing ourselves. At one of these "happenings", in the summer of 1972, Sunshine was killed.'

'You mean she was murdered,' put in Jef cheerfully.

'*Maybe*,' Maddy shook her head. 'It was only called murder later. What apparently happened was that she cut her throat, because of a stage effect that went horribly wrong.'

'Oh,' said Jef, sobered.

'No one could prove that her death was anything but an accident. Of course they tried. All the parents of Bradfield, whose kids were being led astray, would have loved to see Steve and Mike unmasked as nasty criminals. There were the usual rumours. These hippies had been holding court like demon kings: experimenting with drugs, dabbling in the occult … But it happened right on stage, and the weapon – it was a razor – had been used in a way that made it clear she'd been holding it herself. No one had a convincing reason why she would kill herself, though. It turned out at the autopsy that she definitely hadn't been taking any drugs. She hadn't even been drinking. She'd always claimed she never used drugs at all –'

'Pop stars have to say that,' remarked Jef cynically.

'Yeah, well, in her case it seems to have been true. Anyway, she died in full view of the "happening" crowd, so how could she have been murdered? Her death was put down as a freak tragedy. That was the end of *Steve, Mike and Sunshine*. Steve and Mike moved away. A year later they were in Manchester, both trying to start again in the music business, and another girl died. She was Mike's girlfriend. She was found in his flat, with her throat cut. Apparently another suicide.'

'Two dead girlfriends: begins to look like carelessness,' muttered Jef the irrepressible.

'Okay, so we have two suicides,' went on Maddy,

frowning at him. 'Six months' later, a girl's body was found in a shallow grave on the moors outside Bradfield. The police discovered that she'd been auditioning as a singer for a rock and roll band. One of the members of this band turned out to be Mike, from *Steve, Mike and Sunshine*. He'd moved back to Bradfield and was using a different name, trying to live down his past. Obviously the police were suspicious. They questioned Mike, and he denied everything. Then they tracked down Steve. He said he'd been nowhere near Bradfield at the time, but they found traces of the girl's blood in his car, and some bloodstained clothes hidden in his flat ... At which point Steve confessed to *three* murders. He said he'd killed them all: Sophie "Sunshine" Raeburn; Rose Ashleigh and Nadia Khan. He was tried and convicted. Mike was convicted as an accessory to the third murder. He got a light sentence, because it was held that he was under his brother's influence. They put Steve away for a long time, even though they couldn't prove how he'd killed the first two girls.'

'Is that it?' asked Jef, after a long silence. 'A hippie nutter murdered three wannabe girl pop-stars?'

I was thinking of the den under the stage. They had names now, the people who had put up those posters and decorated 'Aladdin's cave'. Steve, Mike and Sunshine ...

'We don't know that Steve killed anybody,' stated Maddy.

Jef and I glanced at each other. 'What do you mean?' asked Jef, slowly.

She stared at us angrily, as if unable to believe we couldn't see what was so clear to her. 'I mean there's something wrong. Steve confessed, how convenient. But if you read these cuttings, you'll see that there's no way he could have killed Sophie, not on the evidence that's given here. Or the second girl either.'

'The police don't give all their evidence to the papers

and the TV,' Jef pointed out. 'Anyway, maybe he *didn't* kill them. Maybe he blamed himself for the first two deaths, went off his rocker and started doing it for real.'

'I don't think that works.'

'I don't understand what you're getting at, Mads.'

Two spots of bright colour had appeared on Maddy's cheeks. Her eyes flashed.

'What I'm getting at is *this*, Jef. Three girls were killed, and a murderer had to be found. Very conveniently they managed to pin the deaths on a hippie pop-star. Let me tell you a bit more about *Steve, Mike and Sunshine* … They were beginning to get some attention. Their style was off-beat, people found their songs kooky and strange. Does that sound familiar? I found a silly interview from a music paper. Do you know why they called themselves *Steve, Mike and Sunshine*? They say, Steve says, that it's a stop-gap, until they think of a really cool name. Does that sound familiar? Don't you see? *It could have been us* … These were three people exactly like us, our age, doing what we do.'

Jef began to play an imaginary violin, his flying elbow causing alarm at the next table, where a couple of Mums were gossiping while their babies snoozed in their floral print buggys. 'Shall we find Sophie's grave and put flowers on it? Let's keep things in proportion, Mads. Life goes on, as that bloke on the radio said, the day Lennon was shot –'

Maddy was determined to make us see. 'Remember the way Dave Ramsey behaved? He was weird about the Powerhouse, right from the start. He knew about this old business. He didn't want us to rehearse there, and he didn't want to tell us why. That's not like Dave. The normal thing for him to have done would have been to tell us the story, not made a big deal of it, just let us know the facts. Why didn't he tell us?'

'Because he's afraid of the Bradfield Mafia,' quipped

Jef. 'Harry Steel told him he'd put the Heavy Heart out of business if he didn't keep quiet. Or is the Lord Mayor too obvious? All right, it was Ms Dangly Earrings. She doesn't want those nasty murders surfacing now, when she's got her techno-nun installed and everything, and she offered him a suitcase full of used Arts Grant money to keep quiet.'

Maddy scowled at him. 'You think it's funny. Well, I don't.'

She took another sheet of paper out of the folder, and pushed it into the middle of the table. It was a copy of a photograph, a black and white print. It wasn't very good quality. We all looked down at the three faces. The blonde girl smiled at us, her eyes big and black-rimmed, trimmed with false eyelashes thick as sea-urchin spines. The two young men both had shaggy dark hair to their shoulders. You could tell they were brothers, they had the same high cheekbones, straight brows and twinkling eyes. One of them was obviously the younger. That must be Mike. They were three nice faces, confident, and full of life. You could see, even in the grainy print, that Sunshine had been very pretty. She had a kind of glow.

'She called herself "Sunshine Ray",' said Maddy, softly. 'Her real name was Sophie Raeburn. I found this photo in Dave's old files too. She was sixteen in that picture. I told Dave what I was doing in the end, by the way. I don't like going behind people's backs, not unless I have to. He didn't like it, but finally he said maybe if I knew what there was to know I'd be able to leave it alone. Only I don't believe I know everything, and I can't leave it alone.'

She drew a long breath, like someone about to jump into deep water.

'I don't know what I'm looking for. But I know there's something: some secret that has been kept hidden. I want to find out what really happened.'

—— 72 ——

Something about the way she spoke, and the strange expression on her face, frightened me. She put her hand on the table, closed in a fist. She turned it over and spread her fingers. There was a key lying on the palm.

'After we found the undercroft door open,' she explained, 'and found all their things in there, I borrowed Sister Kathleen's keys from her overall pocket. I checked which one fitted that lock, and had it copied. I believe the answer's in that room.'

'Wow,' said Jef, impressed. 'You bold girl!'

I was impressed too, but not in a good way. I could understand her sneaky investigation of Dave Ramsey's files: that was fair enough. But I was shocked that she had taken Sister Kathleen's keys without asking. I suppose it showed on my face.

'Don't look at me like that, Robs,' she said quickly. 'It's not the sort of thing I'd usually do, but this is important. We have to use any means necessary.'

Somehow, her explanation didn't make me feel better.

The meeting broke up then. That was on Monday. For a day or two I didn't see either Maddy or Jef. School kept us apart, and we had no rehearsal dates planned that week: Sister Kathleen had the Powerhouse fully booked from Monday to Thursday. Then Jef stopped me on the way out of school on Wednesday, and told me to come to the Powerhouse on Friday evening, usual rehearsal time. He didn't say why, but we never rehearsed on Fridays, so I could guess we were going to do something else. I thought Maddy had more revelations, perhaps she'd discovered letters, or a diary or something. Or else we were going to search the undercroft again.

The Powerhouse seemed to be empty when I got there. The big hall felt different. It had changed almost miraculously once, like a magic trick: from a derelict shell to an arts centre. Now it was another place, a scene of violent death. What kind of a stage effect? I wondered. What could Sunshine have been doing, that could lead her to *cut her throat* by accident? I looked up at that Frankenstein hook and pulley, still hanging in the dome, and shivered.

We never went into Sister Kathleen's studio area when she wasn't there. But I was drawn towards the stone steps. I went up, slowly, into the domain of the burial mounds. 'Easter Rising', 'Immortality' and 'My Heart Is Like A Singing Bird' had been joined by several other constructions, Sister Kathleen's own work and the projects of the different groups that she was working with. They were surrounded by placards explaining who was doing what, photographs of the workshops in progress, high-sided plastic trays full of tubs of goop and tubes of pigment. Some primary school children had been making 'world-boxes', miniature immersions in open-topped shoeboxes. These mini creations were tucked into niches in a hollow stepped pyramid, that was being painted mostly blue, with swirls left transparent ... it must be meant to be lit from the inside. Everything was still. I hadn't switched on the studio lights, and the projects were spooky company. They seemed to be staring at me. I looked at her worktable. I wondered, if I stretched my arm across the litter, would I find that column of cold air? I felt certain that it was still there. And perhaps it stood over the place where Sophie Raeburn had died.

There was a noise from somewhere under my feet. A secret, furtive rustling.

'Who's there?' I shouted: suddenly filled with panic.

Someone laughed. Of course it was Jef and Maddy, they were under the stage. I hurried down the steps. Maddy was standing at the open door. 'Come on,' she whispered, though there was no one to hear. 'Come in, and keep it quiet. We're getting things ready.'

She was holding one of the swathes of fabric from the fancy dress basket, something black and heavy. Jef was wearing a stoved-in top hat and a ragged, mildewed Chinese dressing gown. He was waving a giant crêpe paper daisy. The undercroft was uncannily bright. Maddy and Jef had collected up all the hippie candles and lit them. I saw the skull in flames, a toadstool, a group of rainbow-striped cones. We'd cleared the rubbish and swept away the dust, but we'd never lit candles before. I thought the hideaway must look the same as it had done twenty-five years ago: full of mystery and colour, the eyes of the pop-idols staring boldly down from the walls. They were burning some incense too. There was a prickly scent in the air, and thin wreathes of smoke rose from a brass buddha holder on the brick-and-plank bookcase.

I saw the candles and smelled the incense before I realised that Maddy and Jef were not alone. There were three other people in the dim room, three figures around the coffee table in front of the sofa, heads together, with their backs to me. The girl in the middle had long, light blonde hair. My heart jumped into my throat.

Next moment, the blonde girl stood up and turned round. It was Alanna Cosgrove, a girl from Maddy and Jef's year in our school. The other two strangers were West Bradfield sixteen year olds as well. I recognised Justine Devises and Zeynel Yucesan, both of them Alanna's friends. The three of them glanced at me, shrugged and looked away.

'Stop messing about, Jef,' snapped Alanna. 'Put the stupid flower down.'

'It isn't stupid. I like it.' Jef brandished the dirty old daisy like a rapier. 'I might use it on stage. Like Morrissey in the Smiths, you know, with the gladioli in his back pocket.' He stuck the daisy between his teeth and did a pirouette. 'Gagh! It tastes foul!'

Alanna wasn't interested in ancient rock-music trivia. She rolled her eyes impatiently.

'Can we get on with this?'

I saw, lying on the tabletop, a pack of cards slightly bigger than playing cards, and a glass tumbler. My bewilderment at finding strangers here vanished. I knew what was going on. I'd never played the game, but I'd seen it done plenty of times. There'd been an occult craze, just recently, that went right through the school. Jef and Maddy looked at each other as if each of them was hoping the other would explain. 'Hello Robs,' said Jef, putting down the daisy. 'Glad you could make it.'

Alanna pulled a face, stepped around me as if I was a dog's mess, and went to look at the curios on the brick and plank bookcase. 'Tell the kid what she has to do,' she ordered.

'I hope this is all right,' said Maddy, smiling uneasily. 'You're so sensible, I was afraid you wouldn't join in if I warned you beforehand. Is it okay? Do you want to do it?'

'You're going to have a seance.'

She nodded, with that same awkward little smile.

Well, it was not all right. I was hurt, because Maddy had obviously told Jef what she was planning and neither of them had told me. I could understand why not, considering who it was they'd brought in to run the event, but it didn't make me feel happier. Alanna Cosgrove was exactly the sort of scarey character my parents had been convinced that I would meet when I joined *Hajetu*. She had a horrendous reputation. The teachers hated and feared her. She'd attacked her form tutor with a knife once. She'd been excluded for that; but they'd had to have her back, I suppose nowhere else would take her. Mum and Dad would go spare if they knew Maddy and Jef had me involved with Alanna. They wouldn't like the seance idea much, either. I had not known that Alanna was an expert on the occult. But it made sense. If she didn't dismiss the whole idea as feeble-minded, devil worship was just about her style.

Maddy led me to the coffee table and sat me down on one of the peacock's tail chairs. 'Jef doesn't believe in ghosts,' she told me. 'I expect you don't either. I'm not sure. But the fact is, people have been reluctant to work in this building. It has a reputation. Have you ever felt anything, Robs? Have you felt a presence you couldn't explain?'

I bit my lip. 'Have you?' I challenged.

She didn't answer me directly. 'I think maybe Sophie is here,' she said, hesitantly. 'And if she is, if there *are* such things as unquiet spirits, I think maybe she wants to talk to us.' She paused. 'I wouldn't normally get involved with anything like a seance –'

Alanna, who was still poking around the bookcase, laughed.

'– but it's worth trying,' insisted Maddy.

'So these hippies were supposed to be into the occult,' drawled Alanna, coming over to join us. 'D'you know exactly what they did down here? Did *they* hold seances?'

'I haven't a clue,' said Maddy. 'I don't expect so. It's what people say, "dabbling in the occult". One of those bad things rock musicians are bound to get up to,' she added wryly. 'I don't think the decor means anything. The skull candle and so on: it's only hippie style.'

'Oh yeah?' Alanna produced two more candles, tall and black, that Maddy and Jef had overlooked. 'I think you're wrong.' She sniffed the wax. 'These are not your average fakes. There's power-stuff in them. Not sure what, maybe blood. We'll light them.'

Maddy turned to me again. 'I don't want to make you do this if you don't want to. You can go home if you like.'

Sensible, she'd called me. She meant young. I thought of how I'd reacted when she told us she'd copied key to

—— 77 ——

the undercroft. I'd been like a scared little kid. Compared to Maddy and Jef, never mind Alanna Cosgrove, I was a pathetic baby ... I did not want to be in a seance. I thought they were stupid. I was sure that Alanna and her mates would be in control, and if we received any 'spirit messages' that's where they would be coming from. But in here, the most feeble kind of messing with the supernatural scared me horribly.

I felt betrayed. Maddy had asked me if I wanted to go home. She must know I couldn't back out in a situation like this. She could have told me before, she could have asked me in school ... This is not *like* you, Maddy, I thought. Why are you behaving like this?

'It's fine,' I muttered. 'I d-don't believe in it, but I don't mind.'

'Okay!' announced Jef, unnecessarily loud. 'Are we fit? Let the lunacy begin.'

So we made a circle, cross-legged on the floor, around the coffee table. Maddy and Jef on one side, with me in the middle. Alanna and Zeynel with Justine between them at the other. Justine laid the alphabet cards, and Zeynel took out a notebook. The length of dark fabric that Maddy had been holding lay across the sofa. In the centre of it someone had embroidered, in gold chain-stitch, the letters SMS, intertwined. The velvet was stained and worn, the embroidery wobbly and amateur-ish. I thought of Sophie Raeburn, who had lived here in hippie splendour and cut her throat up on the stage. Alanna balanced the two black candles, in a pair of tarnished silver candlesticks, on the arms of the sofa. The twin flames hung over us, as if they were watching.

'I have to tell you,' announced Jef. 'I think this whole thing's a poor joke. I won't believe a word of it.' He was still wearing his ridiculous costume, the hat tilted jauntily over one eye.

I kept quiet.

'Are any of the three of them still alive?' inquired Alanna. 'I forgot to ask.'

'Not Mike,' said Maddy. 'He was killed in a motor-cycle accident a few years after he got out of prison. Steve served his sentence, I suppose he's out now. I don't know what happened to him. Dave couldn't tell me.'

'Running around free, after killing three girls. That's disgusting.' Alanna jerked an imaginary cord round her neck. 'I believe in capital punishment.'

'Well, I don't,' snapped Maddy. 'It doesn't matter, anyway. *I want to talk to Sophie.*'

Alanna grinned. 'Hey, keep your hair on.'

'Can we get on with it, ladies?' complained Jef. 'I want some ghostly cabaret, if I have to be implicated in this idiocy.' But I saw him give Maddy a puzzled glance.

'Okay, settle down, folks,' said Alanna. 'All you have to do is relax.'

I'd never been involved in a seance before, I'd only looked on. But I knew what to expect. We'd put our fingertips on the glass. Someone would ask questions and it would glide, supposedly guided by the spirit powers, to different letters to spell out the answers. For what seemed like ages we just sat. Fingertips on the base of the upturned tumbler. We were supposed to be breathing deeply and emptying our minds. But Alanna kept looking at me, sarcastically: as if she was wondering why I had to exist. It was a good distraction. I was too worried that I'd do or say something pathetically childish and wrong, to be overwhelmed by fear of the supernatural.

I started to have a feeling that someone else was in the room. Someone was watching over my shoulder, some-one the others hadn't told me about. I was so scared of Alanna that I didn't dare to turn my head: but I had an awful feeling that someone was creeping up behind me.

At last Jef intoned, in a hollow voice: 'Is there any body there????'

Alanna gave *him* one of her 'why do you exist' looks, and said simply, 'Shut up.'

But the spirit guides seemed to be inspired by his question. The tumbler began to move. 'Who's this?' asked Alanna: as if she was talking to someone, in a perfectly normal tone of voice.

S,O,P,H,I,E.

The rim of the tumbler made a nasty little screech, as it skidded round the glass table.

'You don't say,' muttered Jef, with a cynical smirk.

'Shut up,' Alanna told him again.

The tumbler moved.

N,O.

'No, what?' wondered Maddy. 'We didn't ask anything.'

'It means no, it's not going to shut up,' Jef decided. 'It thought Alanna was talking to it. Okay, let's get straight to the point. Who killed Sophie Raeburn, spirit?'

Of course Alanna was supposed to be asking the questions. Zeynel, who didn't have her fingers on the glass and was sitting there with a notebook on her knee, was supposed to be taking down the messages. Alanna glared at Jef. Scared as I was, I found myself choking back a burst of giggles.

At that moment there was a tiny crackling overhead, and the light went out.

'Should we stop while I fetch a new bulb?' suggested Jef cheekily.

I thought Alanna would jump up and whack him. I hoped she didn't have her knife. She only glared again. But the room seemed brighter, not darker. There must have been about twenty-five candles around us. Alanna drew a breath, she was going to speak:

The tumbler moved. It zipped out from under our fingers. Everybody started back, even Alanna. The glass shot around, all by itself, not making a sound now, as if it was gliding above the table top, flying from letter to letter.

S,O,P,H,I,E D,E,A,T,H G,O G,O G,O.

N,O,T G,O, N,O,W, N,O,W, G,O N,E,V,E,R.

I saw Zeynel scribbling down the letters like crazy. I heard Jef muttering: 'Wow, wow, wow. Class act!'

I saw that one by one the candles were going out, until there were only the two tall black ones still alight. I prayed they wouldn't go, because if they did I knew I was going to scream … Then something happened on the sofa. A light formed there. It was clear white and fuzzy and roundish. It rose from the spot where those three initials were clumsily embroidered. The glass tumbler had been racketing round so fast it had flown off, and vanished somewhere down on the floor. The white light rose. There was a buzzing in my ears, or else coming from the light, I couldn't tell. Suddenly it shot into the air and burst into coloured globules, red and green. I don't know how many there were. They flew out like spray from a fountain and dived around the room, hitting the walls and spinning back, whirling over our heads. There was an eruption like a silent explosion from the dressing-up basket. Clothes – braided jackets, velvet skirts, lacy shawls – went flying. One of the thigh-high boots sailed over our heads. The table began to shake. It tilted to one side, then to the other. Suddenly a storm of what seemed like yellow snowflakes filled the air …

That was when I saw something peeping up at me, from under the coffee table. A little face. I don't know, maybe I imagined the face. I had the impression of a wicked little animal, with the most evil bright eyes.

This impression only lasted for a split second.

The table fell back into place. The red and green globules vanished. The light came back on. For a last touch, the two black candles suddenly both fell over and went out.

The other candles did not relight themselves. After a moment or so we all started breathing again, and pulling ourselves together. The show seemed to be over. Jef began cackling loudly. Zeynel and Justine both burst out gasping and swearing they'd never seen anything like it. Alanna didn't say anything. She got up and went to fetch the tumbler. It hadn't broken. It was lying intact on the concrete floor, by the empty dressing-up basket.

It was only then that we realised Maddy had fainted.

She was down on the floor beside me, her legs bent under her and one arm flung over her face. For a moment I was more scared than I had been yet. But as soon as Jef shook her shoulder gently, she roused herself. She sat up, pushing the hair out of her eyes.

'What happened to you?' demanded Jef.

'I-I don't know.' She looked around muzzily. 'I think I fell and hit my head. Is the seance over?'

She tried to stand up, and sat down again quickly. 'I feel sick.'

Alanna and Justine took over, suddenly transformed into paramedics. 'She could have been in a trance,' said Alanna briskly, standing over Maddy, and making her put her head between her knees. Justine felt her pulse. 'Can you get her a drink of water?'

I started to pick up the scattered alphabet cards. I wanted to look under the table again, but I didn't dare. Then I realised that I could hear somebody walking about, outside in the lower hall. The others were taken up with Maddy, they didn't seem to have heard anything. I stood there shaking. Someone was pacing the floor, up and down.

'*There's something ... I mean somebody's outside.*' I whispered.

I said it again, louder. At last they noticed me. We all crouched, stiff as statues, listening to the footsteps. No one said a word. I had a crazy idea that we should fling ourselves behind the sofa and hide.

The door opened. It wasn't a ghost. It was Sister Kathleen. She stood looking in, the big white-walled brightly lit hall behind her.

'Oh, hello,' she said. 'It's you, is it. I thought I heard something going on in here.' Her voice sounded false and strained.

None of us spoke. Sister Kathleen came into the room. 'You've cleaned the place up grandly,' she remarked. 'It's a weird old den, isn't it.' She picked up something that was lying on the floor. It was Jef's daisy: or what was left of it. The head had been pulled off. I realised that the yellow snowflakes had been daisy petals. Sister Kathleen put it down again.

We hadn't spoken to Sister Kathleen since the cleaners had caught us out. We'd been avoiding her, without actually discussing why. But I was sure Mrs Ogden and Mrs Turner would have told her how we'd managed to find the door open, and how they'd locked it again. I was certain she was going to bawl us out, and demand to know how we'd got back in here. She was the one who'd given the cleaners strict orders that we weren't to have the key. But she didn't say anything like that.

'I was just passing the building … I came in to fetch something, and heard noises in here. I thought we had a break-in.'

She sounded as if she was apologising, but I felt that she was really very angry, and trying not to show it. I had a distinct feeling that she knew exactly what we'd been doing. She knew what we'd been doing and naturally she didn't approve. I thought she was going to lecture us about dabbling in the occult, and I felt like laughing hysterically. What would she have thought of the show we'd had in here, just a minute or two before she opened that door?

'Maura Ogden told me you'd been investigating our basement. We often have a chat and a cup of tea when we're working at the same times. Sheila, that's Mrs Turner, has a bad back the same as me. That's why Maura does all the heavy work. They knew you'd been exploring, because of all the dust and dirt you brought out with you. Well, I can understand your curiosity. I did have a peek in here myself, when we all moved in. But it's not my thing, the hippie scene. I thought I'd let the past lie.'

She was staring hard at the alphabet cards, which I'd left in plain view.

'Your man Dave let me in on the old story, the day after that half-baked reception. That poor young girl, with all her life ahead of her. No wonder nobody had the heart to go through these things. I thought I wouldn't pass it on. Young people like you, you shouldn't be worrying yourselves about things that are over and done. But I suppose you were bound to find out sometime.'

Alanna heaved a big fake sigh: like she couldn't endure this old bag much longer.

'Sister Kathleen,' said Maddy. 'What are you getting at?' She was sitting on the sofa now. I wondered if Sister Kathleen could see how pale she looked. 'Why didn't you want us to come in here? I mean, it's none of your business. We aren't doing any harm. There's no reason for you to interfere. Leave us alone.'

Her voice sounded harsh, unlike itself. I wanted to apologise for her rudeness. But Sister Kathleen didn't seem to notice anything wrong.

'Don't you mind about working here?' I asked. 'Aren't you frightened?'

'Of working in a place where a young girl died?' She shook her head. 'I thought it was very sad, that's all. It's lovely to be young, and full of yourselves. It's a shame it had to end that way, whatever was behind it. A shame for all three of them. I've been praying for her, and for the young men too, especially when I've been working with the children and young people: and I've been hoping she rests in peace. But you can't expect old heads on young shoulders.' She shrugged and smiled. 'You young people have a different reaction, I can understand that.' She hesitated. 'I'll leave you to your … your game.'

She was gone. As soon as the door was shut, Alanna burst into loud, rude laughter.

'She has no right,' whispered Maddy. 'She has no right to interfere. Let's wait, and see if she leaves.' So we waited. All was quiet outside. We didn't hear footsteps leaving or the front doors opening. Sister Kathleen's silent disapproving presence, somewhere close by, prevented us from even discussing what had just happened. In the end we decided to admit defeat, and go away ourselves.

I say 'we', but I wasn't included. It was Maddy and Jef, with Alanna and her friends, who sat whispering about Sister Kathleen. I was left out, completely. I took the velvet cloth from the sofa and folded it, and set the table straight. There was nothing hiding under it now.

Maddy and Jef, Alanna, Zeynel and Justine stormed out of the Powerhouse, shrugging on their jackets and talking loudly. When I left them, which was as soon as I could without showing that I was upset, they were still laughing and gasping and shuddering about the spectacular results of the seance. Jef was demanding to know how Alanna did the roman candle effect. Justine and Zeynel were screeching at him for daring to doubt Alanna's genuine psychic powers. Alanna was telling Maddy she must be a natural medium.

It was still early. I'd arranged for my dad to come and pick me up, at the usual time that our rehearsals ended. I called home and told them I was coming back on the bus.

I was convinced Alanna must have set up those special effects. What had happened was obviously fake, how could it possibly have been real? Jef and Maddy were in on the joke. They had to be. But why? As far as I could see, I was the only person they'd been trying to trick. I was almost relieved, because a fake seance seemed to mean there couldn't be a real haunting. But I couldn't understand why Maddy and Jef had been so nasty to me.

Five

I HAD A DREAM THAT NIGHT. A CROWD OF PEOPLE,
Maddy, Jef and Alanna Cosgrove in the forefront,
were standing looking up at me, laughing cruelly. Maddy
was grinning, saying '*You should have seen your face, when
those disco lights went whizzing round the room. You nearly
wet yourself, didn't you ...*' I realised I was on the stage in
the Powerhouse. Something made me look to the side of
the stage. I saw that my friend the rat was crouched
there, the creature I'd often seen in the real Powerhouse:
a little dark thing, with bright eyes. I thought it was
offering me a way to escape.

My friend the rat, that nobody else could see.

When I remember that time it's hard to believe what
my priorities were, after the seance. I should have been
terrified. I should have realised that we'd done something
horribly dangerous. But I didn't. I was convinced that the
others had played a trick on me. I didn't ask myself how
the spectacular effects had been produced. I didn't *care*
how they'd done it. I was too hurt and shamed by
Maddy's betrayal – especially Maddy's – to think about
anything else.

On the Saturday afternoon, as I walked up our front
drive coming home after a music lesson, I noticed three
pairs of scuffed trainers, topped by three pairs of saggy
socks, sticking out from under the cypress hedge. Tom,
and Jerry and Nicholas, I guessed.

'What are you doing under there?' I asked.

'It's our den,' came Jerry's voice. 'Come in and see it.'

I crawled in. The den had a floor of empty peat-free compost bags, and walls of cypress. They showed me the secret passage to the Campbells' garden next door, the tool room where they kept an old hammer, a blunt screwdriver and some nails; the kitchen, and the bedroom, where the Campbells' old dog was asleep on a very dirty rug. Space was limited. In fact, there wasn't much you could conveniently do under the hedge, except sit in a row. So we sat.

'It's not bad, is it?' whispered Jerry. (I knew why he had to whisper: a den has to be secret.) 'Today, we're going to put up some shelves. You can help if you like.'

I wished the Powerhouse had turned out more like this. If only things had stayed the way they'd been on that first day. No fancy new arts centre, no tainted hippie treasure trove, no secret history. If only it could have been just Maddy and Jef and me playing house like kids in a derelict building. It would have been fun …

I forgot that, even on that first day, the Powerhouse had already been tainted.

We were supposed to be rehearsing on Monday evening. It took all the courage I could muster to go along there as if nothing had happened. I walked into the Powerhouse, steeling myself: bracing myself to laugh as loud as the others over the way I'd been taken in by the fake seance. Maddy and Jef were setting up the machines.

Maddy still looked pale.

'About what happened on Friday –' she began.

I gritted my teeth. 'What about it?'

'We've decided to quit communing with the Beyond,' said Jef.

I shrugged. 'Fine.'

'We're going to stay out of the undercroft too, so Sister Kathleen won't be frightened by our ghostly adventures.'

'She doesn't believe in ghosts,' I said. 'She told me so.'

Jef shrugged. 'Okay, she doesn't believe in ghosts. But for whatever reason, she doesn't want us in there. If she catches us again, she might do more than give us a patient little talking-to. It's stupid to risk getting kicked out of here.'

'Just for a while,' broke in Maddy. 'To give Sister Kathleen a chance to cool down. If she's on the alert all the time we'll have no chance of finding out anything.'

I wondered why they didn't simply admit what they'd done.

Maddy stopped in the middle of putting up the Gesture Wall.

'What was that?'

'What?' Jef demanded.

'I thought I saw something running across the floor. It's gone behind that screen.'

'Must be Robs's rat.'

We hunted, but we didn't find anything. The rehearsal went quite well, considering: but Jef and Maddy seemed to be out of sorts with each other. At one point Jef made some remark about Alanna Cosgrove's talents at putting on a psychic cabaret, and Maddy snapped at him. 'It was nothing to do with Alanna, and you know it!'

I made myself very busy trying out some colour chords on the Gesture Wall, and let them get on with it. Maddy and Jef were not boyfriend and girlfriend. Maddy had once told me she'd made a decision never to get involved with anyone in the same band. But I sensed undercurrents between them sometimes. I wondered if the fake seance had been Alanna and Jef's idea. Maybe Maddy had wanted me along for moral support. But I didn't ask any questions. I didn't want to get involved in anything private that was going on between Jef and Maddy and Alanna.

A couple of days later, Alanna Cosgrove actually

stopped me in a corridor in school, and demanded to know when we were having the next session.

'I dunno,' I told her. 'It's nothing to do with me. You'll have to ask Maddy and Jef.'

She rolled her eyes savagely. 'Jef is a wimp. And Miss Perfect Maddy Turner's another. Creeps, losers, what a waste of time. You tell Jef I want to talk to him, and soon.'

Needless to say, I didn't tell Jef anything.

That was the last time we talked about the seance, for a long while. I remained convinced that somehow it had all been faked. I didn't know what Maddy and Jef were thinking. I suppose – assuming those amazing results were genuine – Alanna had a right to be astonished that we didn't want to try again. But I don't think it was so strange. A real encounter with supernatural forces is different, totally different from any kind of spooky playing around. Even if I refused to believe that what had happened was real, I was still very shaken; and so were the others, though I didn't know that at the time. It was the last time we went in the undercroft for weeks, too. We didn't discuss this. The idea of exploring in there was just quietly dropped.

But Maddy stubbornly went on with her investigation. She'd turn up to rehearse with new facts about the case, and insist on telling us what she'd unearthed. She discovered that *Steve, Mike and Sunshine* had actually cut one single, but it had been recalled when the tragedy occurred (record companies felt different about gruesome publicity in those days: imagine that happening now). She found that Sunshine's freak accident rated an entry, (number 19) in a list of *Twenty Strange And Obscure Rock Deaths*, in a book of 'Rock Lists' that she'd found in Dave Ramsey's office. She told us that Steve and Mike Wakefield had begun their career as a guitar

duo called *Wakefield and Wakefield Limited*, in 1968 ...
We listened, but I wasn't very enthusiastic and neither
was Jef.

She *did* make us look for Sophie's grave. We spent one
Sunday afternoon prowling Bradfield cemetery in the
rain, after failing to get any help from a cross man in the
office who said no we couldn't search the register of
burial plots and who did we think we were, private
detectives? So we set out hunting, in the faint hope that
we'd be guided by Maddy's intuition and find one right
headstone in all the marching rows. We didn't.

Sophie Raeburn wasn't buried in Bradfield. She was
buried in a village out in the country, where her family
lived. But I didn't find that out until much later.

We had another gig, which didn't go well. It wasn't
spectacularly bad, but definitely not as good as the ones
we'd done before. We were despondent about that. It's
hard to be professional about a poor performance when
you are starting out. We had an interview in the local
paper, the *Bradfield Evening News*; another in the town's
listings freesheet. The newspaper journalist was moth-
erly, and wrote us up in a very irritating way: *three young
people with a fascinating hobby* was her line. The zine was
fun. We begged them to ask us things like *what's your
favourite colour, what do you wear in bed,* real inane pop-
star questions. They did, and they printed it all! I still
have that issue of *The Information*, with its blurry photo
of Maddy in her false eyelashes and seventies beige
make-up, Jef in his Clark Kent suit doing a demented X-
files stare. We were megastars for the day at school, when
it came out.

But revision for the GCSE exams had engulfed
Maddy and Jef. Both of them were determined to do
well. *Hajetu* would have had to take a background role
this term, no matter what. It was natural that I saw much
less of the other two. The gap of years between us had

opened up again. I thought the friendship was ending, and I felt lost.

One Saturday in May I went to Maddy's house. She'd asked me to make some rehearsal tapes for her, so she could practise her vocals during the breaks in her gruelling schedule. I was delivering them to her at home because she hadn't been able to catch up with me in school. The Turners lived quite near to us, in a street of smaller semi-detached houses. Maddy's father opened the door.

'Oh, hello Robs. I suppose you want to see Maddy.'

They must have been having lunch. I could hear dishes clattering in the kitchen, and Maddy's mother shouting at her. 'But what do you want a nose-ring for? So your boyfriend can lead you round on a string? I'm disappointed in you, young lady. I never thought you were the submissive type.'

'It's *fashion*, Mum,' answered Maddy's voice. 'Everybody's getting it done.'

'They're having a fight,' said Mr Turner unnecessarily. 'I think my cooking disagrees with them. They always fight over the washing up when I cook. Do you fight, Robs?'

I hadn't been in this house often. Mr Turner only talked to me as if he knew me because he was used to having Maddy's friends around all the time. She had so many. I went into their front room. Maddy's little brother and sister were playing a computer game. That is, Eddie was playing the game, while Flick (who was five, and a bit of a monster) kept squirming in under his arms and jabbing maliciously at the keyboard. Mr Turner's newspaper was lying on the sofa, the TV was chatting idly about horse-racing. Three friends of Maddy's, older girls I vaguely recognised from school, were sitting talking to each other and looking at their watches. There was the fizzing of a lot going on: something you never felt in my house. Maybe it was the lack of space, but I thought it was Maddy's energy that filled the atmosphere. Her artwork was framed on the walls, and it wasn't pathetic stuff only parents could love, either. A glittery costume she was making for *Hajetu* was spread over two chairs by the sewing machine in one corner. The sunlight caught in its folds, and shot beams of gold and rosy light through the air.

'There can only be one!' said Mr Turner, picked up Flick, spun her around in the air and tucked her away neatly under the dressmaking.

I sat on the only free chair. Maddy's mother came in from the kitchen, marched up to me and took hold of the end of my nose. She turned it one way, then the other.

'I thought so! Not a sign! So where is this "everybody"? Show me "everybody"!'

'I have a nose-ring, Mrs Turner,' said one of the girls who was waiting for Maddy. 'I take it out for school. It doesn't do me any harm.'

'Yes, but you're a fool Lizzie. This.' She tapped my head, 'is a clever person.'

Lizzie laughed, not at all offended. I thought clever, like sensible, was another word for far too young. 'All right, fine,' said Maddy, appearing from the kitchen, in a shocking pink leather miniskirt and a green satin shirt. 'I'll finish my exams, get pierced and leave home. Then you'll be happy, I suppose. I won't shame you in front of the neighbours.'

'For sure. Good riddance. Until you come back with your dirty washing.'

'You have pierced ears. You told me you had that done when you were *a baby*.'

Mr Turner hid behind his newspaper. Flick crawled out from under the glittery material, dislodging paper pattern and cut pieces. Maddy yelled at her. Maddy's mother got up and went to look at the computer. She leaned over Eddie's shoulder and started saving lemmings, much to his loud disgust. 'Leave it alone, Mum. I can do it myself!'

At last Maddy saw me. Her face lit up. She must have really wanted those tapes.

'Why didn't you *tell* me Robs was here?' she demanded. 'Lizzie, Ruth, Jem: I can't come out right now …'

Her mother started to argue that she shouldn't work all the time, or she would get stale. Maddy ignored her. She fixed up where she was going to meet the others in town later, and dragged me off upstairs. 'This place is a mad house,' she shouted, as we left the room. 'I can't hear myself think, I can't have any kind of private life.'

On the stairs I tripped over the Turners' cat, a black cat called Slim. He liked to skulk in dark places and startle people. Maddy picked him up and carried him into her bedroom, talking all the way about how she was going to get a nose-ring, and a navel-ring, and her mother couldn't do anything about it. She tossed Slim on to the bed, where he immediately rolled on his side and began to fight with the duvet. Maddy went to her dressing table and bent over it, peering into the mirror.

'Oh no. How awful, I *can't* get a nose ring. It's going to ruin the look of my seventies make-up. That's terrible. If I don't get one now, my mother will think she owns me.'

'Maybe it could be an ironic nose-ring.'

Maddy burst out laughing, and dropped back onto the bed.

'You're amazing, Robs. How d'you think of these expressions? When I was your age I was completely feeble minded. I couldn't think of anything but ponies and boy-band hunks.'

I had never been in Maddy's bedroom before. It was small, cluttered and full of light. The wallpaper, what you could see of it, was plain green and white stripes. But most of one wall was covered by a huge pinboard that she had made into a crowded collage of her life: birthday cards, postcards, lapel buttons, lists, notes from friends and boyfriends, a wreath of dried wild flowers, a corn dolly, a sparkly pillbox hat fixed on pins. The best of her antique clothes collection was hanging on the other long wall, displayed like pieces of art. There was a desk stacked with school textbooks, her folders, and heaps of papers closely covered with Maddy's neat, graceful handwriting. A mobile of pebbles and bottle glass hung from the light fitting. I suppose it was what any lively sixteen-year-old girl would keep in her room, but to me it didn't look ordinary. My room at home was at least twice the size of this one, nicely decorated and comfortable. Yet it was empty. I didn't live there. I'd be ashamed to copy her, I'd rather die than do anything so crass. But how I wished I could be like Maddy.

Then I saw, in the middle of that noticeboard collage, a face I recognised instantly. It was Sophie Raeburn. It looked as if it was taken from the same publicity shot that Maddy had shown us in that cafe in Bradfield, before the seance. But this was a glossy print of Sophie's face, clipped out and blown up alone.

'I've brought you the tapes,' I said.

I couldn't help staring at the photograph. I was shocked. I wasn't surprised that it was Sophie up there. Sophie was definitely the one Maddy was most interested in. But I thought of her waking up and seeing that picture of the girl who had cut her throat, the moment she opened her eyes. I knew she was still investigating but this seemed extreme.

Maddy was sitting on her bed, hands clasped. She bit her lip. 'Oh yeah, the tapes. Thanks. Look, Robs, it wasn't really the tapes I wanted. I want to talk to you. Sit down, please. You look as if you're about to walk out.'

I sat on the edge of the chair at her desk. Slim had got

under the bed and was stalking something there. It was hard to see him, a black cat in black shadow. But his eyes glinted.

'It's about the seance.'

Another shock. I thought we were over that business. I'd longed for her to own up to playing a joke on me, but now I knew it would be hideously embarrassing if she did.

'I've really got to go.'

'Jef thinks that it was all faked, all the weird effects. Do you agree with him?'

'Well —' I didn't want to talk about it — 'well, yes.'

Maddy grimaced. 'For heaven's sake. You aren't *thinking* straight, either of you. I mean, Alanna Cosgrove! I actually think she's pretty intelligent, she's simply not interested in school work. But she'd have to be some kind of technical genius, which she isn't. I know, I'm *certain*, that she had never been in that room before she walked into it with me and Jef, about ten minutes before you arrived. Jef couldn't have done it, I couldn't have done it: you know we're both hopeless at technical things. You didn't even know we were planning a seance. That leaves Alanna. And when did Alanna and her mates have a chance to set anything up?'

I knew that Maddy wouldn't take a joke this far. It dawned on me that she was being perfectly honest, and that it was true, I *hadn't* thought it out.

Maddy jumped up and went to her desk, grabbed a sheet of paper. 'Read this. I made Jef write this for me yesterday, I'll explain why in a minute. He promises that's exactly what happened, as far as he can remember. Do you agree with his account?'

I read, while she watched my face. As far as I could make out — Jef's handwriting was atrocious — he'd seen the same as I had. Except for one small thing he hadn't mentioned, it was all there. The tumbler shifting around on its own. The lights, the fancy dress clothes flying through the air, the torn daisy petals, the rocking table … The hairs on the back of my neck started to rise, and my mouth went dry.

'Yes, this is right. As far as I can tell.'

Maddy's eyes widened. 'I wish I'd done this when it happened,' she complained. 'But we none of us wanted to talk about it, did we. If you ask me, that's another proof that what we experienced was real. This is not a game, Robs. This is *scarey*.'

There'd been a stink in school when I was in my first year, about 'dabbling in the occult'. Some parents had complained after a sleep-over party that had collapsed in screaming mass hysterics. Our headmaster had discovered that there were a lot of ouija board sessions going on, and declared a clamp down. Since then, though people were still fascinated, the craze had gone underground. But I had never heard anything that made me believe for a moment that there was anything in it. Not until now. Suddenly, I knew that Maddy was right. I had convinced myself that I'd been tricked, because the alternative was too frightening. We had gone into the Powerhouse undercroft with our stupid alphabet cards and silly *is there anybody there?* questions … and we'd woken something real and monstrous.

'What do you think we should do?'

'I have to trust you and Jef,' said Maddy, seeming not to have heard my question. 'Because I was unconscious. I don't remember anything after the glass spelled out "SOPHIE", "NO" and Jef asked who killed Sophie Raeburn. I heard that question, and then I woke up on the floor.'

She leaned forward, arms around her knees, her eyes intent and dreamy. 'Sophie Raeburn was there,' she said, very softly. 'She was there, when I … I wasn't. She was trying to get a message through.'

She stared at me, challenging me. I stared back, uneasily, until I had to look away. Slim's bright eyes glinted at me from under the bed.

'You don't believe me,' stated Maddy. 'I can see you don't. I know it's hard to accept. Okay, let me show you why I'm sure.' She took that card folder from her desk, the one I thought of as the Sophie folder, and shook out some slips of paper from an envelope.

SOPHIE NO SOPHIE DEATH GO GO GO
NOT GO NOW NOW GO NEVER

'Those are the words the spirits spelled out for us at the seance, aren't they. Now see this.' She took out a greyish scrap of lined notepaper that had been torn from a spiral pad. Typical Maddy, she'd put it neatly in a transparent plastic envelope. She handed this to me and I read, puzzled, an odd list of phrases:

Forests of the Mind
Singing Branch
P-P-Passion Killer Baby
Do Black de Black
Gentleman Mr D'Eath
Sweet Sweet Heartbeat Lies

'What is it?'
'I found it under one of the peacock chairs, when we were cleaning the undercroft. Don't you recognise it? Those are song titles. It's a prompt list. She had that taped to her guitar, on stage, to remind her of the playing order in a set. Remember, we found a guitar.'

I remembered the guitar, the acoustic guitar we'd found. The neck was cracked, the box smashed-in, and the wood was badly stained inside and out. It had been a cheap instrument to start with, it wasn't worth repairing. We'd chucked it in a corner with the rest of the workmen's rubbish; with the carousel horse and the canvas tree. I thought of those dark stains with sudden horror. I noticed, again, how much Maddy had become focused on Sophie. It had to be Sophie's guitar. Sophie's prompt list.

'And now, listen to this …'

Maddy leapt up again, and went for the tape deck on her big battered ghetto–blaster. There was a cassette already in the slot. She wound it back and switched on. I heard a lot of buzzing and crackling, and then a thin, small whispery voice, without accompaniment. It seemed to come from very far away.

'*Take me to my lover, take me now or never, Mr D'Eath* …'

It sounded like a ghost singing.

'That is Sophie Raeburn,' said Maddy, solemnly.

I gaped at her. '*How* –?'

'I found it, at the Hungry Heart. You see, when I confessed to Dave that I was investigating what had happened to *Steve, Mike and Sunshine*, he made the mistake of telling me he thought he had an old Revox reel-to-reel tape recording of them somewhere. You know the loft at the Heavy Heart, that Bradfield Music Scene landfill dump in an attic? It was up there. I pestered him until he tracked it down, and begged him to make a copy that I could play. He gave it to me yesterday. There isn't much. The quality is awful. But that's *her*.'

She switched off the cassette but the solo voice went on, very softly. For a moment I didn't know where it was coming from. Then I realised that it was Maddy, singing.

'And there's more.'

She searched through the folder, lost patience and tipped out all the Sophie papers on to her bed. She scrabbled among them, and grabbed something triumphantly.

'Here it is. This is an eyewitness account of Sophie's

death. It was the twenty-first of June 1972, the summer solstice. It was the Press who called it a "happening". The people who were there simply called it a free concert. *Steve, Mike and Sunshine* were on stage. That means up in Sister Kathleen's studio area. It was late, about one o'clock in the morning. They were doing their second set. You can imagine it, can't you. That big space, but not white and bright the way we know it: all murky and mysterious. Packed with people. Everyone who had the chance for miles around, everyone on the scene who knew about the place was there. Sophie and Steve and Mike were actually living in our hippie den at the time.'

She snatched up another piece of copied newsprint. 'It says here *"Sophie Raeburn had left home, much to her parents' distress. The three had been secretly holding court in a derelict building where the local youth came to pay homage, to dabble in drugs and, it is rumoured, to take part in strange rituals"*. You see, they were there full time.'

Maddy gazed at me, but it was as if she was looking into the past. 'They were on stage. Everyone was dancing, most of them in fancy dress. Mike and Steve had rescued the sets and props from a church hall production of *Carousel* and distributed them around the hall. It was dark in the pit (that's our rehearsal space), except for the candles in the sconces, but the stage was strobe lit. The person who gave the eye-witness account – it's anonymous – says everything was confused. He admits he was using drugs himself that night. He says they were doing *Gentleman Mr D'Eath*. It was a song about a boy who dies in a car crash, and his girlfriend decides to kill herself: she falls in love with death. Sophie was singing. Steve and Mike were looning around behind her, identically dressed in black and masked. One of the brothers, playing *Gentleman Mr D'Eath*, was supposed to hand a fake cut-throat razor to Sophie, like a present

—— 100 ——

from the devil. It was from a joke shop, the prop that is. But that night the razor was real. All they knew in the audience was that suddenly Sunshine Ray had collapsed. They didn't know the blood was real. This guy says, he didn't positively see either Steve or Mike hand the knife to her. But it was impossible to tell what was going on, because of the strobe. He says: "*I was dancing with a tree at the time. I didn't know anything was wrong. The music stopped and we were being asked to leave, that was all. I went and lay on the grass in the Wild Park for a while, then I went home. I didn't know Sunshine was dead until I heard it on the news the next day ...*" Mike and Steve both said they *didn't* hand Sophie the razor. Not that night. She had it herself all along ... do you see what I'm getting at?'

I shook my head. I was mesmerised by the story itself, and by the way Maddy seemed to know it off by heart.

'The words at the seance. They're the words of that song, *Gentleman Mr D'Eath*. The one she was singing when she died.'

'I suppose they're quite like them,' I agreed, trying to calm things down.

Maddy's eyes flashed. 'It's the identical words! You have to admit that!'

She frowned. 'The razor only had her fingerprints on it. Mike was a biker. It must have been parts of his motorcycle that we found in the undercroft. He loved wearing biker gear, the black leather and the Hell's Angels accessories. They took a big knife that belonged to him and tried to prove he'd cut Sophie's throat with that, and stuck the bloodstained razor in her hand to make it look like suicide. But it didn't match the wound.' She looked up at the photograph on her noticeboard. 'There's something about her being in a strange mood for a few days before that night ... I can't remember which of them said it, either Steve or Mike. But I can't believe she killed herself. She doesn't *feel* to me like someone who would kill herself. She was a perfectionist. Maybe she'd decided the joke shop razor looked stupid, so she'd switched it for a real one – and then her hand slipped. But I don't believe that. I believe there's something else. *Someone's* lying, in all this evidence. Don't you feel that?'

'What about the other girls? I can't remember their names.'

'Rose Ashleigh and Nadia Khan,' supplied Maddy promptly. But she was still gazing at Sophie Raeburn's pretty face, and the intensity in her voice suddenly dropped: she was only interested in Sophie.

'If both of them, Steve and Mike, were in love with Sophie, one of them could have killed her in a jealous rage. That's what the police suggested ... But she wouldn't have been playing them off against each other, she wasn't that sort of person. She would have held things together. No, I don't believe any of the explanations in this evidence. There's something that isn't here. Something vital, that has been missed out of all these reports. And I'm going to find it, I have to find it ...'

I was liking this less and less. I had a sinister feeling that if I read those news cuttings, I'd discover that they didn't have half the details Maddy seemed to know. She was making things up, maybe without even knowing it. She was getting obsessed.

'If they'd been a little further down the road to success,' she murmured, 'they might have become famous when she died. People are such ghouls. But they weren't, they were only local heroes. Like us. So they vanished as if they'd never existed ...'

'That's why you're interested, isn't it?' I broke in. 'Because you think they're like us.'

Maddy laughed at the word I used. 'I'm more than interested, Robs. I feel as if I'm being driven. I have to do whatever Sophie needs me to do. It's as if she's trapped, and I have to free her. It's getting between me and my work, I don't mind telling you. I come up here. I try to revise. It's no use, my mind just goes Sophie, Sophie, Sophie.'

'I don't understand. You can't make them famous now.'

'I know that. Maybe she just wants someone to know the truth. Whatever it is.'

She started to pick at a lock of her curly hair, pulling off the split ends. That struck me as odd: it wasn't a Maddy-gesture. She wasn't a fidgety person. But it was all of a piece with the rest. None of this was like Maddy. I felt hopelessly inadequate. I'd had no idea that the investigation was having such an effect on her. Maddy was my idol. She'd always been so strong and wise.

'Has Alanna asked you about having another seance?' she asked abruptly.

'Well, she did once.'

'Thought so. She's been pestering me and Jef as well. Says I'm a natural medium, and the Powerhouse is charged with psychic energy. Look, I don't want Alanna involved. Will you promise me you won't talk to her about any of this?'

'Of course I won't.'

'And I don't want you to talk to Sister Kathleen either.'

'About what?' I faltered, bewildered.

'Say you promise. I need to hear you say it.'

'I promise,' I said. I'd have promised anything, if Maddy would only be Maddy again.

She nodded in satisfaction. 'Sister Kathleen's the enemy,' she remarked, thoughtfully, as if we were both agreed on this obvious fact. 'Do you realise, Dave must have told her the whole story, that first Sunday morning. Yet she didn't say anything to us. I think that's very weird. And look at the way she accidentally came by the Powerhouse, that Friday night when we were in the undercroft.'

'I think she knew,' I blurted. 'She knew what we were doing, and she didn't like it at all. She was trying not to show it, but I think she was very angry.'

'You're probably right.' Maddy scowled. 'She knows we're trying to reach Sophie, and she's determined to stop us. Well, we'll simply have to be careful.'

'About what?' I quavered.

She looked at me solemnly. 'I want another seance, Robs. I've been wanting to try again for weeks, only I was sure you and Jef wouldn't agree. But when I heard that tape … I knew I'd have to persuade you somehow. I don't want Alanna there. I don't want any of that letter-cards and fingers-on-the-glass nonsense. It has to be you and me and Jef by ourselves. And … and Sophie. Please tell me you'll do it. I don't think Jef will agree unless you're going to join in. He's such a coward.'

Slim the black cat was asleep on Maddy's pillow. I noticed this, with a start. I was sure he'd still been under the bed a moment before. I'd been aware of that distracting, animal movement in the shadows all the time Maddy had been talking. I shook myself, and rubbed a hand over my eyes. *It's all too much, I thought. I'm as bad as Maddy. She's obsessed with a dead pop starlet and I'm seeing things.*

Maddy was gazing at me imploringly. I had been afraid our friendship was ending, now Maddy was telling me I was the only person who could help her. I desperately did not want to be involved in another seance. But what could I say?

ii

All I could do was pray that the second seance would soon be over. The three of us would shut ourselves up in the undercroft and call on the spirits. Nothing would happen, I *prayed* that nothing would happen, and the spell would be broken. Maddy would realise she'd been getting unbalanced about Sophie Raeburn, and everything would be back to normal. Maddy had convinced me that we had witnessed some genuine paranormal phenomena during that other session; but I told myself that didn't mean it would happen again. Didn't everybody say that paranormal events were random and unreliable? The very fact that we'd had such a bumper crop of effects first time probably meant we were safe from ghostly phenomena in the undercroft for the next hundred years. *Lightning doesn't stike twice in the same place* I kept telling myself. *It won't happen again.*

Maybe it's true that lightning doesn't strike twice. But if you stick your finger in a live power socket, you'll go flying across the room every time, no matter how often you try. I think I knew this. I knew the danger. I was the one who called that place the Powerhouse, after all. But I was doing it for Maddy. I had to help Maddy to lay the ghost of Sophie Raeburn, and this seemed to be the only way.

And I was so afraid of being left out.

As often happens when there's a crisis situation in your life, as soon as I'd agreed to take part in seance number two, the urgency vanished. Sister Kathleen was very busy trying to get all the groups' projects finished in time for the exhibition. She seemed to be in the Powerhouse day and night. Jef got Maddy to agree to wait until revision hell was over. He tried to get her to wait until the end of the exams. She resisted that firmly: but I began to hope we could go on finding excuses forever. After the Residency and the exhibition, the Powerhouse was going to be closed for 'further refurbishment' until September. I was sure that the long summer break would make everything different. If Jef and I could only hold out for a few weeks longer, we might be safe.

One Saturday on my way to music class, I went there

by myself. The doors were unlocked. I slipped into the lower hall very quietly. The nun-artist was up in her studio, working. I could smell melted plastic. I watched her for a moment, and realised she wouldn't hear me whatever I did. She had a walkman tucked into her overall pocket, and phones in her ears. I stared at the spectacle of a nun wielding a blow-torch, wearing a dust mask, an eyeshield and a personal stereo. Then she looked around: switched off the torch, and pulled down her mask. 'Robs,' she shouted. 'Hello!' She yanked out the earphones and said in a more normal voice. 'Why don't you come up here?'

I went up the stone steps.

'I haven't seen much of you three for a while,' she remarked cheerfully. 'We should get together more. Are the others coming this morning?'

Her friendly tone was rather false. We'd hardly spoken to her since the evening she'd caught us in the under-croft. Relations had been strained.

'No, they're not coming. I was just passing by, and thought I'd drop in.'

Sister Kathleen gave me a sharp look, then pretended to be really interested in the melted patch of surface she'd been working on. But I knew she was watching me closely out of the corner of her eye.

'These project deadlines are getting me down. I never have time to work on my own pieces ... I know it isn't you,' she remarked next. 'Which of them is it, that's so interested the dead girl. Is it Jef, or Maddy?'

'It's Maddy,' I said.

Yes, I broke my promise. I think some promises deserve to be broken. As Sister Kathleen had already guessed, I'd come here hoping to find her. I had to talk to someone.

'Ah.' She nodded, as if her guesses had been confirmed. 'The poor child.'

I didn't know if she meant Maddy or Sophie. Maybe she meant both.

'How did you know?'

She pursed her lips. 'Ooh, I had a glance at a certain notebook. You could say I've been spying. But in a good cause.'

'It's like an obsession,' I burst out. 'Sister Kathleen, do you think anything's wrong with Maddy? She keeps thinking about Sophie, wanting to find out more about her death. She seems to feel as if she *knows* Sophie. She says Sophie's in trouble, and that we have to make contact with her ghost. It scares me.'

'And do you think you *have* made contact with the ghost?' asked Sister Kathleen, in a non-committal tone.

I couldn't stop myself from blushing.

'We sort of tried,' I admitted. I didn't think I was giving anything away. 'But you know that. That time when you found us in the undercroft. I'm not sure if we made contact. Some strange things happened, though. We saw lights flying about. And the table rocked. And the candles went out.'

'Is that a fact,' said Sister Kathleen mildly.

'Don't you believe me?'

'I believe all sorts of effects can be …' She paused. 'Well, it doesn't have to be deliberate fraud. I believe if a group of people gets together determined to have a spooky experience, they'll probably have one.'

'I *didn't*, though,' I protested. 'I definitely didn't want to see anything!'

She stood back: picked up the torch from her work-table, put it down again, and picked up a craft knife. 'You've big circles under your eyes, Robs. You haven't been sleeping well, have you? You know, when ye're young, you never think of the simple explanations. You and Maddy and Jef, all three of you have been working too hard. With this band of yours, and all your school work. You're doing too much, and just when ye're out-growing your strength. Give yourselves a few weeks of regular meals, early nights, calm days. You'll see no more rocking tables and flying lights.'

'You don't believe in ghosts, do you? You don't think people can contact the dead.'

'I do not. Not by playing conjuring tricks, anyhow.'

'So – so you think it's all our imagination.' I felt extremely relieved, even if I wasn't completely con-vinced. 'But what about Maddy? What can I do?'

'Maddy's a good girl,' she said. 'She's a level head on her shoulders.' She frowned at the plastic shell, as if it had the whole problem written in its lumpy folds. 'I don't like any of that hocus-pocus you were trying: but if it was Jef I'd be more concerned …' She put down her knife, sighed and turned to face me. 'You want me to tell you how you should deal with your friend?'

I nodded, wondering why she looked so stern and angry.

'Well, I can't do that. If I must advise you, I have to admit you'll probably do more harm than good by fighting with her, or pouring scorn on what she believes. If she feels you've let her down and goes off on her own tack, that could be worse … I'm getting nowhere with this fellow,' she added, changing the subject with finality. 'I'm very bad at finishing things. I like to fidget with them forever. Come downstairs, and I'll make us a cup of tea.'

I went on to my music lesson feeling puzzled at Sister Kathleen's attitude: but reassured. It seemed as if I'd made the right decision. We would have the seance, nothing terrible would happen, Maddy would get back to normal.

Unfortunately Sister Kathleen herself was in the way of this happy ending. She'd told me to go along with Maddy's ideas, but something told me she wouldn't approve of another full scale session trying to contact

Sophie's ghost. And she never seemed to leave the Powerhouse now. It was as if she was on guard.

Mrs Cosso let me in, and returned to the weekly chore of refreshing the bowls of pot pourri she liked to keep on every surface. She didn't care for fresh flowers (too messy). But she loved rich scents. She continued to glide around on her little doll-slippers, like a whale on tiptoe, dispensing her drops of warm oil and stirring up the bowls. The air was filled with Woodland Garden and Elizabethan Pomander. I played some scales, and then began to pick out a tune. I recognised the melody of Sophie's fatal song, and quickly stopped.

'Do you believe in spiritualism, Mrs Cosso?'

'Talking to spooks? Messages from Great Auntie Mabel on the other side? Not at all! It's all fraud and hysteria.' I'd forgotten that Mrs Cosso's arch rival in the bridge circle, a fearsomely well-preserved old lady called Helen Washington, was a big fan of the spirit world. She annoyed Mrs Cosso by telling fascinating tales about famous mediums, and distracting the other ladies from Mrs Cosso's own dazzling anecdotes. 'Fraud and hysteria,' she repeated ferociously. 'Don't ever have anything to do with those people. Now *palms*. That's different. I have the utmost faith in the laws of palmistry.'

I'd had my palm read. Mrs Cosso had discovered I was going to be a great artist, have three children, and would always have a tendency to weak ankles. Terrific news.

She looked at me suspiciously. 'What's the matter with you this morning? Why all the chit-chat? Stop trying to pull the wool over my eyes, and play me something.'

So I played Chopin, feeling reassured again. But as the notes flowed from my moving hands, I thought that Sister Kathleen and Mrs Cosso were both wrong. As I played, I asked and the composer answered. I understood why Frederic Chopin had done this, and not that, chosen one way, and not another, as if he was here beside me, teaching me, instead of Mrs Cosso with her lace blouse and magnificent ice-cream bosom. We knew the same craft, we used the same language. In the ordinary world he had died, but in the music he was alive. He could speak to me and I to him.

It seemed like fate when Mrs Cosso mentioned that the nun-artist was going back to Birmingham, to her Community house, for several days next week.

'Are you sure?'

'Of course I'm sure,' she snapped. Mrs Cosso became very annoyed when I doubted the pinpoint accuracy of her gossip. 'I heard it from Ivy Deacon, the sister of Maura Ogden who cleans your art centre, same time as she told me the nuns on the estate have had their car broken into for the third time this year. They took the radio again, and some clothing the nuns were collecting for a jumble sale: imagine that! They never take the car itself, the old thing's such a rust bucket ... Sister Kathleen will catch the early bus to London at the Limited Stop by the Wild Park gates on Wednesday morning. I hope it doesn't pass her right by,' she added darkly. 'As those drivers have been known to do. I've seen it from my window.'

'I only wondered, because of her deadlines. She seems never to leave her studio, she's so busy preparing for the exhibition –'

'Deadlines, pah. Deadlines aren't everything. An artist must have a Life. Besides, she's obliged to go back, I think. It's some feast day of theirs, some Roman Catholic ritual.'

Of course I had to tell the others. We agreed to meet as if to rehearse, as usual, on Thursday at half past six. It was the sixth of June.

Maddy was late. Jef was alone when I arrived. Maddy had the copied key, so we couldn't get into the undercroft. It was a strange moment. It wasn't something I thought about or noticed much, but I was hardly ever alone with Jef. We stood and looked at each other. Apparently neither of us could think of anything to say. Jef began to prowl around the hall. He had his arms wrapped round his skinny chest and his hands tucked in his armpits, as if he was cold; though it was a warm evening. He stopped by the pile of copper pipe that still lay along the wall by the passage that led to the kitchen, and kicked at it idly. The metal sang.

'I had my French oral today,' he said suddenly.

'Did it go okay?' I asked politely. It was very odd to think that they were both in the midst of those terribly important exams.

'I talked. I constructed fluent idiomatic sentences – I hope. I made French-ish noises. But I was thinking about this damned seance.' He scowled. 'Why did that nun have to go home? I can't afford to have spooks on my mind at this crucial point in my brilliant career. I'm embarrassed to be part of this business. I think it's unspeakably stupid. You haven't read any of that stuff in the folder, have you?'

I shook my head. I'd managed to avoid this.

'Well, I have. I've examined the evidence. There's not a hint of a secret conspiracy, or a cover up. It's all in Maddy's head. Can't *you* talk to her? You're the posh one. You're little Miss Perfect. She'd listen to you. Why don't you tell her it's *simply not done?*'

He put on a fake fancy accent, supposed to be like mine. I didn't take offence, it was only Jef. I understood that Maddy was right, he *was* afraid. Those cheeky comments at the last seance had been Jef trying to keep up a macho front, when he was actually terrified. I was very surprised. I was scared too, but then I was so much younger, and Jef was always so brash and bouncy. I thought of telling him about lightning not striking twice, but it suddenly didn't sound like a strong argument.

—— 111 ——

'She wouldn't listen to me any more than you. We have to let her get this out of her system. We have to go through with it. It'll be all right.'

Jef shook his head. 'I wish I was sure of that.'

Then Maddy came into the hall. She was almost invisible behind a huge mass of florists' wrapping paper. She was also carrying her radio cassette player. She struggled to shut the doors and turned to us with a happy smile, her arms full of flowers.

'What's this,' demanded Jef. 'Been raiding the cemetery?'

'Don't be nasty, Jef. They're for Sophie. No cracks about funerals, please. I'm going to try and create a different atmosphere. I don't want this to be a creepy seance. I want it to be beautiful. You two look in the kitchen and find me some vases, jugs: anything like that.'

Jef and I went to look for vases. We didn't talk any more, except to compare our finds, and discuss whether Maddy would be satisfied with empty milk bottles. Then we all went into the undercroft. The air smelled of snuffed candles and incense, because it had been shut up since the Alanna session. Jef and I hung about uncomfortably while Maddy tried to create her 'different atmosphere'; until with an air of bravado he sat down on the sofa, pulled a vintage *Sandman* comic out of his pocket and began to read. I found myself plumping up the cushions on the peacock chairs, the fussy way my Mum always plumped cushions, the moment any one had disarranged them. The dust that was still buried in there, decades deep, floated out and made my eyes water. I did not see Jef turn a page.

'There!' said Maddy at last. 'What do you think?'

She'd filled about ten vases, bottles and jugs, with masses of flowers. They stood on the brick-and-plank bookcase, on the floor, on the filthy old paraffin heater, on the crate of pots and pans. They were lovely. But maybe there were too many, or maybe the light was wrong. It was gloomy in here, even with the door wide open and evening sunshine streaming in. Somehow they didn't improve things.

'Surreal,' declared Jef, unsympathetically. 'Definitely surreal. Not unlike a seventies LP cover, come to think of it. We could call it *Dead Flowers In The Satanists' Den.*'

'This has nothing to do with Satanism!'

'Oh no? I thought you'd talked to Dave Ramsey. Didn't he tell you about what really went on in this place, twenty odd years ago?'

Maddy scowled at him. 'I don't believe everything Dave says. He's a gossipy old woman. He invents things to keep up his funky reputation.'

She took out some matches and started lighting candles.

I went to close the door, but Maddy stopped me.

'No! Leave it open. I told you, I want this to be different. It's quite safe. Nobody's going to burst in on us this time.'

She smoothed the black velvet cloth over the table, and set her cassette player by the embroidered initials. She placed the two black candles one on either side.

'Jef, you and Robs sit in the chairs. I'm going to be here.' She pulled up that mould-encrusted leather pouffe to the other side of the table. 'No cards, no corny ritual, no stupid questions. Just us, thinking of Sophie.'

'What if nothing happens?' asked Jef, swopping seats with a resigned grin.

'Then we'll know that she's at peace, and we'll go home. Then I'll be satisfied.'

Dust motes drifted in the sunshine that poured in through the open door, connecting this fusty den with the world of light and air. I had taken a dislike to the black cloth, and wished Maddy hadn't used it. I didn't like the way it covered the table. Anything could be hiding under there, secretly watching us. But I didn't want to slow things down by making difficulties. *Think about Sophie*, she said. I wasn't planning to think of anything in particular. There ought to be a time limit on this session. How long should we wait, I wanted to ask. Half an hour? An hour?

But Maddy had switched on the cassette player. It had begun.

'We're going to imagine ourselves back there,' she told us reverently. 'Back to that night in June, in 1972. We're going to think about what we know and let the pictures form in our minds. We're going to recreate that night, and find out what really happened …'

The tape hissed. We heard a man's voice, quite loud. *Is it switched on?* he asked. Another male voice, it sounded like somebody different, laughed. A chord, jarringly out of tune, twanged from an acoustic guitar, and a palm was smacked against the soundbox. *Start again*, ordered the voice that had laughed. The tape hissed. The first young man's voice began to sing, over some simple chords and a rippling melody: *doodoodaadaa silver branch and summer tree, doohdooh daahdaah there's a goblet filled with secret wine.* A girl's voice joined him in harmony. The singing and the guitar music gathered strength: it went on for a while. It was a terrible recording. But even if the tape had been better, my musician's instinct told me there was nothing much going on here. Maddy wanted to believe that *Steve Mike and Sunshine* had been on the brink of fame: that was part of her obsession. Maybe it was true. But there wasn't much proof of their talent in this feeble relic.

'I guess you had to be there,' drawled Jef.

Maddy whispered, 'Sssh. It's coming next.'

Oh Mister D'Eath, sang Sunshine Ray in a breathy, little girl voice.

Be mine tonight.

Don't stand me up, not like my other boy

Sophie Raeburn, Sunshine Ray. I wondered what she was like, the girl who ran away from home to join a rock band: the sort of thing I wished I could have the nerve to do. But I wouldn't be able to run far or stay away for long. The raggle-taggle gypsies probably wouldn't keep a baby grand in their camp. I wouldn't be able to practice. What could you make of a girl who called herself Sunshine and sang songs about 'Mister Death'. She must have been a crazy mixed up kid.

He let me down, now I depend on you

Because I can't, can't see the light of day

Can't see his face, unless you take me there

I understood how Maddy felt about Sophie Raeburn, because it was almost the same way I felt about Maddy. I admired everything about her. She was the person I wanted to be; and it could be that I admired her too much. But with Maddy and Sophie it was more than admiration. Maddy was losing her grip on reality. Look at the way she'd forced me and Jef to take part in this performance. She didn't seem to *care* that we weren't interested, to put it mildly. Didn't it matter to her that we hated what she was doing? If Sophie's spirit was really hanging around the Powerhouse, trying to get a message through, it'd be a miracle if she succeeded. She surely wouldn't be getting any help from me or Jef.

Take me now or never, Mister D'Eath …

The memory of our first seance came back to me: the strange lights, things flying through the air. Could it have been all somehow caused by wishful thinking, our imagination? I hoped so. *Fraud and hysteria*, I repeated to myself, comfortingly. *It's all fraud and hysteria*. The tape had stopped. With luck that meant we could soon go home. *Get out of here and never come back*, I thought. By the time Maddy and Jef had finished their exams, Sister

Kathleen's Residency Exhibition would have begun. The Marquee would be up in the park, we'd be able to rehearse there ...

These were the thoughts, or something like them, that were going through my head. I kept praying that Maddy would say it was over, so I could get out of this gloomy atmosphere, away from the sickly scent of the flowers. But none of us stirred. I almost wished we *were* performing some kind of eerie ritual, because I felt so empty inside. It was like being in a dentist's waiting room, only a million times worse. I didn't dare to look at Jef. I guessed he was feeling much the same as I was. Maybe I *should* look at him, and give him a hint that it was time to break things up.

I didn't move a muscle. I was sitting in the peacock chair, bolt upright, hands on my lap. They felt as if they were heavy as lead. Then I felt as if my hands weren't there. I couldn't feel any part of my body, it was as if I was floating inside a tank, not touching the sides anywhere. *Is this a trance?* I thought. I began to panic, but I could not move.

Fraud and hysteria, I kept repeating silently, desperately, *fraud and hysteria!*

Nothing had changed, nothing but this strange immobility. Then the door very softly closed. I couldn't turn my head, but I could see it out of the corner of my eye. It didn't shut completely. It stayed a little ajar, a beam of dim light falling through the gap.

'Don't move,' whispered Maddy, her voice shaking with excitement. 'I think we've made contact! Don't either of you dare move!'

She didn't know I couldn't.

There we were, the three of us, grouped around the empty sofa, as if we were talking to someone who wasn't there. Maddy had arranged us like this.

'Sophie?' she murmured, like someone coaxing a child.

'Sophie, I have a strong sense that you're near us. Are you here?'

I heard a scratching overhead, a slow deliberate scratching. Something was trying to attract my attention. Next there was a whole series of little scurrying sounds. That was the rat, my old friend the rat, running across the stage overhead. I could see it in my mind's eye. Now it was dropping from one step to another of the stone steps. I had a taste in my mouth like the water from dead flowers: a coppery, electrical taste, but foul too. I remembered, suddenly, the thing creeping under Maddy's bed. I'd thought it was Slim the cat. But the cat had been asleep on Maddy's pillow. I wanted to shout a warning, I was trying to shout out: *We've been led into a trap! It's not Sophie's ghost that's haunting this place!* But I couldn't move and I couldn't speak.

Maddy gave a deep sigh.

There was a figure coming into shape on the empty sofa. It began as a shadow, a shadow thrown from nowhere. It grew from the feet up, until it was human-sized. Then it shifted: like a candle unburning, like smoke turning into wax, from formless darkness into pallid colour. It was a girl. She was wearing a long creamy–coloured dress, with a square neckline and trailing open sleeves that fell among the folds of her full skirt. Her blonde hair framed her face in smooth waves. She was sitting with her legs tucked up, holding an acoustic guitar across her lap. Her face was blurred, as if there was a veil over it. But I could see her black-rimmed eyes, and the outline of her lips.

'Sophie!' whispered Maddy, her voice trembling. 'Can you speak?'

The rat-thing was scurrying across the floor of the lower hall. Out of the corner of my eye, I saw something blocking that ray of golden light. A small dark shape crept into the undercroft, behind Maddy: a presence like

—— 117 ——

an animal, but it moved with too much purpose to be an animal. I saw eyes, gleaming bright. I was terrified that it would come and jump on me. I didn't think I could bear that. It hopped and skittered over the wreckage of the paper daisy.

'Can you tell us what happened, Sophie?' Maddy was asking. 'Is that what you want us to know?' She was leaning forward over the table, as if trying to catch the dead girl's breathless confession. 'Take us back there. Show us what happened, that night in June. You didn't want to die, did you?'

Jef shouted 'Don't touch her, Maddy. Don't!'

The face looked at Maddy. I saw its empty eyes gleam, I saw the lips stretch in a meaningless smile. The figure lifted its hand, and tipped back its chin. A splash of darkness leapt out of the throat. It spread all over the pale dress. My paralysis broke. I threw up my arms, involuntarily, as if the spattering blood was real. Maddy lunged forward with a loud wailing cry, and seemed to catch the falling body in her arms –

There was a crash. Somebody screamed and screamed. I think it was me.

The door of the undercroft flew open. The overhead light came on, brilliantly bright.

Sister Kathleen yelled 'What's going on in here? What are ye up to, ye three scallions, ye three wicked young divvils!!!'

I found myself kneeling on the floor. Jef was still rigid in his chair. Maddy had crumpled across the table, knocking the cassette player to the ground. Sister Kathleen rushed in, her face crimson with fury. She shoved over most of the flower vases, kicked the candles down and stamped on them, until not one was left alight. She dragged us out of there, hauling me and Maddy by our collars, pushing Jef ahead of her. She shook down Maddy for the key, yelling at us all the time: slammed the door and locked it.

I was so shocked and overwrought I burst into tears. I remember I kept protesting, through my sobs, 'You said it was all imagination, you said it would be all right.'

'I never said anything of the sort!' she gasped. 'Or if I did, I was sorely wrong. That's the end of these stupid games, you hear me? Don't let me ever catch you again –'

'We thought you were in Birmingham,' I explained, my teeth chattering.

She was panting, her eyes still blazing with anger. 'Well then, I was. I came back.'

'We were sitting in the dark,' Jef sounded as if he was talking in his sleep, 'Just sitting in the dark, that was all, because Maddy, Maddy –'

Then I saw that it *was* dark. The tall windows around the hall were black holes in the bright white walls. To me it seemed only five minutes since it had been half past six and broad daylight. I looked at my watch, it was ten o'clock. My dad must have been and gone, he must have come and banged on the doors and had no answer. He'd probably gone to fetch the police.

Sister Kathleen had started to calm down. 'Come in the kitchen,' she said, in a gentler voice. 'I'll make a cup of tea. You can tell me exactly what happened.'

'Nothing happened,' I sobbed. 'Honestly, nothing!' I couldn't bear to talk about it. All I wanted was to get away, wipe this out, pretend everything was all right.

'I'm going home,' announced Jef, still sounding totally bewildered.

Somebody banged on the front doors, rattled the handle and finally got them open. My mother looked in. 'Oh, hello everybody,' she smiled, with a casual air, seeing nothing wrong. 'I'm afraid I'm a bit late Robs, sorry about that. The doors were locked. I've been wandering about trying to find another way in.' I felt weak-kneed with relief. I'd never been so glad to see her. My mother, with her carefully arranged auburn hair, her perfect makeup and her smart office clothes, sent Sister Kathleen into another dimension: dwindled and small so she couldn't bother us at all. 'What about Maddy,' I said. 'Can we give her a lift?'

We all looked around for her. But Maddy had already gone.

Six

I SAW MADDY THE NEXT DAY IN SCHOOL, BUT ONLY
for a moment. I was crossing Lower School reception
with DeeDee, the same place where I'd met Maddy and
Jef the day we found out the shed had been knocked
down. Maddy came in the glass doors and walked by us,
heading for the stairs. She was probably going to an
exam. Some of the GCSE exams were being held in the
Lower School gym. I didn't say anything to her. Don't
ask me why. I didn't look at her, and I don't know why.
But DeeDee, a loyal member of the Maddy Turner
unofficial fan club, piped up. 'Hi, Maddy! Good luck
with the paper, whatever it is.'

She turned her head, smiled at us, and walked on.

Maddy's face. Remember, at the beginning of this, I
tried to describe Maddy's face? It was the same arrange-
ment of features. But what looked out of the eyes …

Maddy went on, up the stairs. DeeDee recovered first.
She caught her breath, and laughed. 'Sometimes you get
days like that,' she gabbled, inanely. 'Bad Smile days.'

I don't know how I survived until the end of school. I
kept thinking of the Lower School gym. The polished
floor laid with canvas. The rows of desks and bowed
heads, the speeding pens, the silence … I thought I must
be going mad. The only cure was to see Maddy again. I'd
have to catch her on the way out of her exam. But I
didn't. Then I told myself I'd call her, as soon as I was at
home. We'd talk about the seance, agree on a story to

keep Sister Kathleen from complaining to Ms Dangly-Earrings, discuss how we could stop Jef from making things worse. Everything would be normal.

I didn't do that either. I went home and shut myself in my room. I came down to have tea, because the last thing I wanted was for Solange to notice there was anything wrong. I didn't manage to eat much. I went back upstairs and stayed there, with the TV on for an alibi. I sat on my bed, and watched the door. A couple of times I thought it began to open. I thought I saw a slanting band of sunlight broken up by a small, animal-like shadow. I thought I saw it creep in, the way it had crept in and sneaked up on Maddy. Once or twice, the dim shape of a pale-haired girl began to form, sitting in the chair in front of my workstation. Between these terrible moments there were long stretches when I sat as if I was paralysed, thinking of what had looked out of Maddy's eyes. I tried to concentrate on something else: the pattern on my wallpaper, the nine times table; anything. I'd succeed for a few minutes, then the bad thought would come stealing back, and I'd find myself trembling. I told myself I had a nasty attack of seance-burn. It was a form of psychic scalding, caused by dabbling in the occult. Really, nothing was wrong. The things I'd seen could be explained. If it wasn't fraud it would have to be hysteria. Overwork, too much imagination, all kinds of comforting excuses. I would feel better soon. On Monday Maddy Turner's face would look perfectly normal to me.

I got undressed and went to bed. I kept the light on all night.

After about six am, I think I dozed. I know I was asleep at seven thirty, when my dad started banging on my door. I opened my eyes and saw familiar things, dull things: my alarm clock, a blue pottery bowl that I kept oddments in. A stack of paperback books, children's stories that I'd grown out of. A small white teddy bear with a green ribbon round its neck. I felt the horror sliding back into my waking mind, taking possession of these innocent objects, filling my boring, harmless room.

Dad stuck his head round the door and said, in tones of deep disbelief, 'There's a nun on the phone for you. Called Sister Kathleen.'

'It's the Artist in Residence Dad. You know about her.'

'Do I? Well, I've forgotten.' He spotted something he didn't like: marched into my room and stuck the jack on the end of my phone lead back into the socket on the wall. 'Don't *do* that,' he snapped. 'We're not providing a secretarial service for you, my lady.'

He was annoyed because he liked having a daughter with a phone in her room, and her own TV, and anything else she wanted. It made them feel pleased and proud to give me things, and it hurt them when I wasn't appreciative. He went off downstairs. I crouched on my bed, thinking in despair how useless it would be to explain to him or Mum what was wrong. Parents like mine are at their best before you're three, I think. When they can dress you up and carry you around showing you off; and they don't have to listen to a word you say. They meant well, but I could tell them nothing.

I had pulled out the phone jack because I'd been afraid Maddy would call.

Sister Kathleen wanted me to come to the Power-house: she said Jef would be there. She didn't say any more, but I felt incredibly relieved. Sister Kathleen would know what to do. I left straight away, as soon as I was dressed. It was a beautiful fresh summer morning. The sky was clear and blue, the Wild Park awash with sunlight and warmth and flowers. When I reached the Power-house I almost couldn't make myself go any further. It stood, surrounded by the bright green of the June woods, full of horrible satisfaction. It had won. I went in, and saw Sister Kathleen and Jef up on the stage. I quickly joined them.

They were sitting at one of the metal tables from the coffee bar area, in front of them two mugs of tea. Jef's head was bowed between his thin shoulders, his hands clasped between his knees. Something was different about the studio, but I couldn't quite place what. Jef looked up as I came near. I'd been hoping – and dreading – that I'd find that I was the one with the problem, that all the horror was in my mind. But I knew, as soon as I saw his haggard face, that Jef and I were in this together.

If only we'd talked more, before the worst happened. We'd let Maddy do all the work of holding *Hajetu* together. If we'd paid more attention to each other, maybe we'd have been able to stop this.

'It's about Maddy,' he told me bluntly. 'Have you seen her, since the seance?'

'Just for a moment. Yesterday, in school.'

'Did you notice anything strange?'

'Yes. I thought she … she wasn't like herself.'

His freckles stood out on his white skin. 'Not herself. That's what I thought too.' He laughed, rather desperately. 'I always hated this place,' he burst out. 'Right from the first moment I thought it was a creepy dive. I never told you two. But I knew.'

'Then why didn't you *say?*' I cried. 'You were the one who insisted we had to work here, when Maddy and I didn't want to. You told us you loved the place. You wanted to have the Festival show in here –'

'I was *acting a part*, you stupid woman. I was trying to be cool. Have you never heard of a person being afraid to be afraid?'

Sister Kathleen said quietly, 'Jef called me yesterday. I went to Maddy's house in the evening. I didn't explain anything, I simply said I had come to see how she was. Maddy spoke to me … I think I agree with Jef, there is something badly amiss. Her parents weren't surprised to see me, they weren't surprised that I should be anxious.

—— 124 ——

They're worried themselves. They told me she's been working too hard.'

'But what *is* wrong?' I pleaded.

Sister Kathleen looked at me, almost warily. 'Tell me what you think of her.'

I couldn't put my feeling of blind loathing and terror into words. I'd have sounded crazy myself. 'It's hard to describe. It's just that it's not Maddy. It's not her at all.'

Jef said to Sister Kathleen, 'I called *you*, because I think you know something. This is why you were so angry when you caught us having a seance. I think you've seen this happen to someone before. Am I right? *Come on, you have to tell us!*'

She looked very uncomfortable. She picked up her mug of tea and turned it in her hands. 'It's cold,' she announced, standing up. 'I'll make some more,' Sister Kathleen and her everlasting cups of tea! But she sat down again.

'All right, no putting it off: I'll tell you. When I was young,' she began. 'When I was your age, Jef, I had a sister. She was older than me by a year and a half. She was a lovely girl. But so gentle, and not stupid but not very clever. She was not strong, in body or spirit, my Mary. The kind they call easily led. I felt I was the older, from when we were very small. I was the one who looked after the younger ones; and Mary too. My sister had a friend, a boyfriend, that was killed in a car accident. They weren't engaged. I wouldn't have said they were serious about each other. But after Billy was killed, Mary cared more about him than she ever had before. She had his picture in her room with flowers round it, like a little shrine. I thought she was putting it on, and I said so. I said she was in love with being a tragedy queen, not with poor dead Billy. That wasn't very tactful, and believe me I was sorry for it later.

'This was in Ireland, long ago. There was a rich old

—— 125 ——

lady lived in a big house outside the town. I wouldn't call her old now, or rich either maybe, but she was impressive to us all then. She had a circle of privileged friends who would go to her house and talk about spiritual matters. Sometimes they had an expert from Dublin or from London come to lecture them.'

Sister Kathleen sighed again. Her bright blue eyes were suddenly dim.

'Now all the grown-ups knew well what kind of "spiritual" matters were discussed at Lady Lisdevine's house, and some people were scandalized. They said she was trafficking with the devil. But she was rich and grand, so nobody was going to interfere. I didn't care anything about it one way or the other until Mary started going to those meetings. She was a pretty girl, and the old ladies took to her. Our parents wouldn't stop her because they thought Lady Lisdevine might "do something" for Mary, find her a good job or a well-to-do husband. I was disgusted. I thought Mary was being taken in. I loved her dearly, but I told her she was a fool. She said she would never speak to me again. And she never did. I went away to college that September. We never wrote. Near to the Christmas holidays my father came to fetch me: we had no telephone. He said Mary was ill. She'd "collapsed" they said, at one of those spiritualist meetings. I didn't know why he told me she was "ill" with such a grim face, because he said she was up and about. I thought she couldn't be so bad as all that. I came home, and I talked to her. I talked to her all one night. But it was … it wasn't my Mary. Oh, that was a bad time. I'll never forget that night as long as I live. She knew none of us, and soon she was violent. They had to take her into the hospital or she'd have harmed herself. My poor sister had lost her mind. She never recovered. She didn't live very long after.'

Sister Kathleen wiped a hand across her eyes. 'The

doctors said what was wrong with her was something called hebephrenia. They said nothing would have made any difference, she was bound to go like that. But I knew it was down to those cursed seances. Lady Lisdevine was distraught about it, couldn't do enough for Mary, swore she'd never allow an impressionable young girl to join the circle again. But it was too late for my sister. D'you remember Jef, you once said I joined the Order as if I was joining the Foreign Legion. To forget. Well, that cut home because you were partly right. I'd been chewing over the idea, that term at college, of being a nun. I was afraid to tell anyone because I knew they'd laugh at me. I wasn't the holy sort. The only person I could have told was Mary, and we weren't speaking. After what became of her: well, that made up my mind.'

'I'm sorry,' muttered Jef. 'I shouldn't have said that.'

'You weren't to know ... So you see, that's why I don't like seances. When I found you three with your friends that other evening, I knew what you were up to. But I was afraid to lose your confidence, the way I did with Mary. I thought I'd just try and always be on hand, and keep a close eye on my keys. I didn't guess then you had a key of your own. When I went up to our House last Wednesday, I was afraid you would take advantage. But I couldn't help it. We run a rest home. One of our elderly ladies had to be taken into hospital, and she was asking for me to be there. It's a very frightening thing, a hospital, when ye're elderly. I couldn't refuse a call like that. So I went back, and I saw her settled. That took up my Wednesday, til late. Thursday last, that was Corpus Christi, is a lovely feastday with us. I'd meant to stay, but then I knew I had to get back here. That's how I came to find you in the undercroft.'

'So that's where we're at now,' whispered Jef, his green eyes huge in his white face. 'Either Maddy's gone mad. Or else she's possessed. The ghost has taken over. Sophie killed herself, and now she hangs around here trying to take possession of some other girl …'

Sister Kathleen looked uneasy but said nothing. Jef glared as if she'd laughed at him.

'Okay, I know. You don't believe in ghosts. In spite of that story you just told us, I suppose you still don't believe. But I know what I saw last night!'

'It is my faith and hope,' said Sister Kathleen quietly, 'that the spirits of those who have died have better things to do than play foolish tricks, or prey upon the living. That's what my religion teaches. I don't believe that my sister made contact with her dead boyfriend, and I don't believe that you three have been talking to Sophie Raeburn.'

'Then what did I see last night? Robs, tell her. I *know* I wasn't imagining things.'

'Does it matter?' I pleaded. I was crying, I couldn't help it. 'Surely what matters is Maddy. How can we help her?'

Sister Kathleen had moved her work table. She had cleared it and pushed it to the back of the stage, in preparation for the exhibition. I was suddenly riveted by this change, tears drying on my cheeks. I didn't hear her answer to my question. The floor of the stage wasn't concrete now, it was thick embossed black rubber. I stared and stared at the space where the table had been.

I heard Sister Kathleen saying: ' … careful, not to talk wildly, make things worse …'

'But we have to decide what we're talking *about*, don't we?' demanded Jef, his voice rising to the edge of panic. 'Should she see a shrink-doctor? Or a priest? How do you organise an exorcism? Is it expensive? Are they in *Yellow Pages*? Who do we call?'

'Sister Kathleen,' I burst out, 'why didn't you want us to go in the basement? If you don't believe in ghosts, why didn't you want us to know about those old murders? I know you were trying to protect us. What were you protecting us from?'

Jef and the nun-artist both looked at me in alarm, as if I'd suddenly gone crazy too. I stood up. I felt sick and terrified; and irresistibly drawn to that sun-filled empty space.

I stepped into the sunlight. 'It's gone.'

'What's gone?' snapped Jef. 'The table's over there. What are you talking about?'

'The cold patch. Like you get in haunted houses. There was a place here that was cold ... and, and horrible. I found it by accident. Sister Kathleen found it too. You did, didn't you? Please, please tell me –'

For a horrible moment I thought she was going to say she didn't know what I was talking about. I was wrong. It was worse than that.

'Yes I did,' she said, grimly quiet. 'And I know the cold is not there this morning.'

Whatever it was that had inhabited the Powerhouse, whatever it was that had made that hateful, mind-eating patch of empty air, it was gone. It had found somewhere else to live. None of us spoke. Jef had already talked about 'possession', but I knew he'd only half believed it could be true. Now I was sure that the horror I had met, on a winter's day that seemed impossibly far in the past, had gone to live in Maddy.

'You said you didn't know we had a key,' said Jef at last, in the voice of someone who's gone over the edge: beyond disbelieving fear into horrible certainty. He sounded strangely calm. 'How did you think we were getting into the basement, then?'

'That door comes open by itself sometimes,' explained Sister Kathleen. 'Whenever I'd found it open, I would lock it.'

Jef started to laugh. 'And after all this you don't believe in ghosts?'

'Maybe I believe in something worse.'

That sobered him. He didn't ask what she meant. I thought of a little creeping thing, like an animal but not an animal. A little thing with bright eyes, that fed on fear and envy, and hunger and loneliness and shame ...

'But what do you think we should *do?*' begged Jef again.

'I'm not sure,' said Sister Kathleen carefully, weighing every word. 'We have to bear in mind that there still may be nothing much wrong. She's not like my Mary was, she's not out of her mind. You two see a great difference in her, but that may be partly because you're over-wrought yourselves. I don't think you should be going to a doctor, or a priest, not yet. We must be very careful. The mind is such a delicate thing once it's in difficulties. Our Maddy is a good strong girl. But if she's been under a lot of strain, and then she's been badly upset by imagining she's been talking to a dead girl, then if we cry "Maddy's crazy!"; or "Maddy's possessed by the div-vil!", we could be on our way to *making* her very ill, even if we're completely wrong. But I've seen her, and I think you've a right to be anxious. Be with her as much as you can. Talk to her, get her to do familiar things: rehearsing your music, maybe. Let's give this a few days. Whatever's happened to disturb her mind, Maddy is a strong person. You know that. She'll be fighting back.'

Jef nodded, looking relieved.

'There's someone I want you to see,' went on Sister Kathleen, after a pause. 'Someone you should talk to about this. I can't bring him here. Could you, one of you or both of you, come round to the Drop-In Centre, maybe tomorrow evening?'

'I'll come,' I said quickly. 'Jef's in the middle of exams.'

Jef looked at me gratefully. 'Thanks, Robs.'

Then we had to leave. Sister Kathleen had a morning

workshop. People had already started arriving, strolling into the new arts centre in their bright summer clothes, chatting about the fine weather.

ii

The estate didn't look as bad as I'd thought it would. Jef or Maddy had always come to fetch the keys when we needed them. I'd never had a reason to do anything other than walk by these blocks of flats, that stood staring at each other across the bare turf and the grimy paths. After all I'd heard from Mrs Cosso I was expecting scenes of post-holocaust devastation: roaming mutants with machine guns, smashed windows, broken doors; old mattresses and burned-out cars. There was *one* burned-out car, and there were some sour looking bored-teen-ager types hanging around. That was all. Mostly it just looked poor. Scraps of litter strayed across the tired communal grass. Dogs wandered, fat mums in saggy teeshirts leaned out of fifth floor balconies and shouted to each other over the shrieking of their children. Nobody took any notice of me. I found the block that held the Drop-In Centre. There'd been an entryphone but it was broken, Sister Kathleen had warned me. The outer doors were wedged shut. You could push one of them open.

Someone had peed in the lift. Not all that recently. The smell was old and faded, and mingled with disinfectant: but I decided to take the stairs. I knocked on the right door. A smiling middle-aged woman let me in. She wasn't wearing a nun's habit but she was dressed in a blue cotton overall with a cross pinned on the front, and her hair was covered by a black sort of snood, with a white band round her forehead. I was expecting some-thing like a doctor's waiting room. She showed me into a sitting room that was decorated neatly in depressing taste: floral prints in lukewarm pastels. There was a desk covered in stacks of papers, office tidy things and a couple of telephones. It had been a dining room table in another life.

Flyers for local community events were tacked up on the wall behind, alongside some doctor and hospital leaflets. Another woman was sitting beside the desk. She was wearing the same blue cotton and snood and she was talking to someone on the phone. Two girls drinking beer were sitting on a sofa watching TV. One of them was nursing a very small baby. The woman who'd let me in asked me to sit down. I looked at the beer-drinking girls. They looked back: not curious, not unfriendly. The woman on the phone said *Yes ... yes ...* and nodded her head sympathetically at the person who couldn't see her. I thought, *this is the Artist in Residence's secret life*. It's strange to see what someone you know does when you're not around: how they live when you are not looking at them.

Sister Kathleen came back with the first woman, 'Hallo Robs,' she said, and started in at once to business. 'Now listen, I'm going to leave you alone with him because otherwise he won't speak. Don't worry, I won't be far away, and he's a gentle soul. I believe he wouldn't harm a fly. You talk to him, and then tell me should we get him to talk to Maddy. Come along through here.' She led me into a kitchen. A man was waiting there.

'Steve,' she announced. I noticed that she positioned herself dead in front of him, as if he was deaf and would have to lip read. 'Steve, this is the person I told you about. This is Robs Hayward, who's been working with me in the new arts centre.' She took my arm and put me in front of him, making sure I too was directly in his line of vision.

I'd been counting on this mysterious 'someone'. I'd jumped to the conclusion that he must be an expert in the supernatural, someone who was prepared to talk about the things Sister Kathleen refused to discuss. I'm not sure what I was expecting. Some kind of Jedi Knight figure: someone like Doctor Van Helsing, the one who knows everything about vampires in classic *Dracula* movies. A saintly warrior or great magician who would give me a swift crash course in vanquishing demons, issue me with my very own sharpened stake and silver bullets. Instead there was this shabby, middle-aged man, thick grey hair hanging to his shoulders, perched on a breakfast stool. He was holding a green and blue pottery mug. His hands and face were raw-looking, as if they'd been scrubbed with a kitchen scourer.

'I just made some tea,' announced Sister Kathleen. 'Would you like some?'

I shook my head.

I stared at Steve Wakefield. He didn't mind, or he didn't care. He let me look. His eyes were dark. They seemed to be set far back in his head, because he was very thin. The rims were swollen and sore looking, as if they'd been burned. They had a tendency to wander, watching something behind you or off to the side. His skin was ruddy and coarse instead of smooth and pale, all his features were grooved, slackened and blurred; there was grey stubble pricking round his jaw. But I could still see the face in the photo. I could even see that he wasn't really very old. If his hair hadn't been so grey, he wouldn't have looked much older than my own father. I couldn't understand how he could have been in that long ago story, and then in jail for a lifetime; and still be here in front of me. I kept expecting him to crumble, like a vampire in daylight, and fall into dust.

'You are Steve Wakefield?'

He nodded slightly.

'Robs wants to know,' prompted Sister Kathleen. 'about you and Mike and Sophie Raeburn. She's not thrill-seeking, she has a good reason. I'll leave you to chat, if that's all right.' She went out, leaving the kitchen door open behind her.

Steve looked at me, his mouth twisted in a sour smile. I understood that he'd been told to talk to me and he'd agreed, to keep Sister Kathleen quiet: but it wasn't his idea.

'Please,' I said. 'It's really important. We found your place, under the stage.'

'You found the den?'

'Yes. It was locked, but we got hold of the key. It was exactly as you left it.'

His mouth went on smiling bitterly, while his wandering eyes slid over to a corner of the room. 'Well fancy that. I don't remember what we left there. The black candles? The crystal ball? No, I think Mike took that. Okay, you want to hear our sad story ...' He peered at me, out of the back of his head, with a glimmer of curiosity. I thought of something broken and shrunken, living far inside a shell that had become too big. 'Sister says you're rock and roll musicians. Is that right? You and your friends, you make electronic music with visuals, whatever that means.'

'I don't think it's rock and roll. Isn't that guitar music? I think what we do is more techno.'

The man with the burned eyes laughed. He put down his mug and took a packet of tobacco out of his pocket. He was wearing an oversized dark blue suit jacket and trousers that didn't match. He smelled like the lift, of disinfectant and recently banished filth: not clean, but cleaned-up.

'Techno. Well, well. I was inside for fifteen years. It puts you out of touch. You look about thirteen. How d'you manage to look so young? Is that through healthy living? Or a pact with the devil?'

'Actually it's nearly true. But I'm fourteen now.'

'And you want to know what we did in the den. Well, fine, here goes. Mike and me found the pumping station, and all our friends started using it as a place to hang out.

Sunny wasn't getting on with her folks. We fixed her up with a room in a flat in town, but that didn't work out. So then we moved her into the den in the basement. For a while we all lived there. It was cheap, and we had no money. It kept the rain off, what more do you need? It was a great secret hideaway. We were like kids, grown-up kids. Everything was great, except between Sunny and her folks. We were going to get a record deal ...' He stopped, looked down at his gnarled sore-looking hands and laughed. He hadn't done anything with the tobacco pouch, he was just holding it.

'I'll tell you one thing. When they wrote about her in the papers, afterwards, they all said *Sophie was such a happy careless child, until those bad hippies lured her away.* That was drek, you know. Complete pie in the sky. She didn't run away to be a pop-star, she ran away because she was desperate. She hated her life at home, really hated her dad. We were the only people she trusted. So she ran away to us. We never touched her, do you believe that? Neither of us. She was like a little kid, it would have been a crime to mess about with Sunny. Do you believe me?'

I nodded. 'I believe you,' I said firmly, because it seemed important.

'We told them she'd been acting strange, before that night. *Strange!* That's no word for it. I couldn't look at her ... made me feel sick. We knew there was something wrong, hellish wrong, but we didn't know what to do. She told me that night there was a maggot in her brain, and I said *Don't be daft, Sunny, you're imagining things.* I told her to snap out of it, and then she cut her throat, right up on stage.'

So she had killed herself. Just what Maddy didn't want to know. But the things he said, the look in his burned eyes, told me that there was more.

'What had happened to make her like that? Do you know?'

Steve glanced furtively at the open door. 'I dunno if I should tell you this.'

'Please?'

'It was so long ago,' he complained. 'How d'you expect me to remember? If you can remember the sixties, you can't have been there. But for us it was only beginning. The seventies were going to be our swinging decade … We had played at making magic Robs. We knew some people who were into genuine black magic. There was one older man … His name doesn't matter – he was well known at the time. I think he's dead now. He drew us in. Weekends in the country, big house, swanky food, midnight sessions in fancy dress with fire and smoke. We thought he was very cool. We learned how to do it from him. But I can't tell you what we did, how we did it. I can't remember: and if I could, I wouldn't tell. You don't want to know, girlie. We conjured something up, one night in the den. We called a spirit and it came. What a lark. We conjured this funny little thing with bell, book and candle. We told it to serve us, and it did. It served us right …'

I had begun to shiver. I could feel the open door behind me. I was afraid that Sister Kathleen would look in and he'd stop talking. My hands felt very cold, and my mouth had gone completely dry. I managed to whisper: 'What did it look like?'

Then Steve Wakefield seemed to look at *me*. Properly, for the first time. Until that moment he'd been trotting out his story automatically, not caring who I was or why I was listening. His expression changed completely. The slack, blurred look vanished, he was Steve from the photo.

'You've *seen* it?' he breathed.

'I don't know. Is it like, a little shadowy monkey? Or maybe a rat?'

'I always look for it,' he said hoarsely, staring at me.

—— 136 ——

'Peeping around corners, creeping on the edge of sight. It's been gone for a long time, but I know it's going to come back. When you think you'll never see it again, there it is. It took Sunny. It will come for me, someday soon. It crawled into Sunny's head, and it wrecked her mind: and then when she was dead, it waited for the next, and the next –'

He stopped suddenly, looking horrified. 'You won't tell Sister?' he demanded urgently. 'It's not safe to tell any of them: shrinks, screws, Sister-Mercifuls. They're nice women, the Sisters, but you don't want to tell anyone about the delusions. You'll end up inside again, padded cell this time, brain-death medication. Oh God, please don't tell them.'

He looked as young as me, and desperately scared. 'I won't tell.'

'Swear?'

'I swear.'

He heaved a sigh of relief; and his face changed again. I felt him go, back into the depths of his shell.

'You didn't kill anyone, did you?' I whispered.

Steve's eyes were looking for something in the shadows of the bright poor little kitchen, where there were no shadows. 'Mike had taken them back there,' he explained. 'Rose, Nadia: he felt he had to show them our den. That was how it must have got to them. And so they died, like Sunny. When he found Nadia dead he panicked. He called me up and told me it had happened again. He'd made such a muck of trying to get rid of the evidence, I had to help him. Hide her, bury her, make it go away.'

'But why did you confess?' I felt so sorry for him. He'd spent fifteen years in prison for a crime he didn't commit, his whole life was a wreck. Maddy had been determined that there was something wrong with the murder trial and she'd been partly right. Steve was innocent. I couldn't understand why he'd done that to himself. 'Did you do it to protect Mike? You didn't have to do that. He was innocent too, surely you could have proved it!'

The burned eyes stared at me. 'Oh,' he whispered, in a voice like dirt and rust. 'You're so wrong. You don't get it. I was the one, you see. I was the conjuror. Mike and Sunny depended on me, and that's what I did to them. I'm oldest. If you're the oldest, you're responsible. Didn't your mum ever tell you that? When I knew three girls had had to die or else live possessed by that *thing*, d'you think I wanted to be free? I wanted to go down. I've been down, but I've come up again like a bad penny. Oh God, I wish it was over.'

He began to cry. He turned and buried his face in his arms on the kitchen counter, hunching his shoulders against me, against the world.

Sister Kathleen slipped back into the room. She touched my arm, and led me out. 'Wait a moment,' she said, and went back to Steve.

The beer-drinking girls were still watching the football. When things got interesting on the pitch, the one with the baby held it up and hugged it and pointed its tiny face at the screen. I thought she shouldn't be drinking beer if she was breast-feeding. I was surprised that the nuns hadn't told her that. The woman who'd let me in was on the phone now. The one who'd been on the phone was talking to a shaky old man in a stained Fair Isle cardie, who'd appeared while I was talking to Steve.

Sister Kathleen came back. 'I'll see you out,' she said.

We walked down the stairs, and met a woman who was washing them. She insisted on giving Sister Kathleen a long telling-off about how soon they'd be filthy again.

'How did you find him?' I asked, when we had escaped from the cleaning lady. Our footsteps went rap, rap, rap in the empty stairwell.

She shrugged. 'I asked around. It wasn't so hard. He's been living round here since he got out of prison, apparently: getting by from hand to mouth.'

'Limpets in a rockpool,' I said.

We'd reached the bottom of the stairs.

'She's doing her GCSEs!' I cried, as if this was the most important thing. 'It's not fair, she didn't mean to do anything wrong. What about her exams? And we're supposed to be playing at the "Marquee in the Park", it's our big break! Sister Kathleen, it's not *fair*.'

Sister Kathleen sat down, on a battered vinyl sofa that had been left in the entrance of the block. She patted the torn seat-cover beside her. I sat down gingerly, avoiding the grey cotton-waste stuff that oozed from the hole.

'Ye're very young.'

'Thanks,' I told her bitterly. 'I had noticed.'

She sighed, 'Well, you've heard Steve's story. He blames himself for all three deaths, and that's why he confessed: but I think he's no murderer.'

'Could you … could you do something about it? Get the case re-opened?'

She shook her head. 'He doesn't want that. We've thought about it, and we've decided it would be just cruel. He's served his time. Working with people like Steve, you learn not to try too hard. Some wrongs cannot be righted. But now we're thinking of Maddy. I don't think she should talk to Steve herself –'

'No!' I gasped.

'No, I thought not. But would it help if you told her you've talked to him?'

I remembered the way her obsession had started. She'd been convinced that there was some kind of conspiracy. A Bradfield conspiracy to protect the real murderer and stick three horrible crimes on a hippie musician scapegoat. If I could tell her that there *was* no secret mystery, that three girls had committed suicide and Steve himself had decided to take the blame ... ? But I remembered the thing that had looked out of Maddy's eyes. I knew that she was not having some ordinary nervous breakdown: and Steve had not been raving when he talked to me just now.

'It would help if it was Maddy I was talking to.'

'Mmm,' said Sister Kathleen. She stared at the floor, squeezing her hard, strong craftworker's hands together. At last she said, 'I had some bad times when poor Mary lost her mind. I thought of devils, possession, awful things. I don't say that it isn't possible. But like I told you, you have to be careful not to do more damage by naming names ... The best I can tell you is that in the end it doesn't make any difference. Ye can call it madness, or ye can call it possession by an evil spirit. Ye can chant invocations and burn incense, or ye can call in a good psychiatrist. The real weapons are the same. There's no magic spell for what ails Maddy, Robs, if she's in that deep trouble. There's only those simple weapons ... if you have the faith and courage to use them right.' Her eyes went bleak and sad. I knew that she was thinking that she had not managed to save her sister Mary.

'What do you mean, weapons?' I was still hoping for a silver bullet.

'Well, love,' said Sister Kathleen, 'you do love Maddy, don't you?'

'Yes.'

'And there's prayer.'

'I don't think I know how,' I quavered. 'I don't believe in God. I mean I do, sort of, believe in something. But I don't know what God is ...'

'Never mind that. To pray means to ask. So ask for protection, comfort, help. Don't worry about who it is you are asking for these things, or where the help will come from. Think it comes from deep inside yourself, if that helps. Just ask: for Maddy, for your self. Call on the Spirit. You won't be turned away.'

I couldn't tell her what Steve had told me. It would be a crime and a shame to break a promise made to someone like Steve. Anyway, she had said *It doesn't make any difference.* Suddenly I knew how frightened I was. Those other girls had killed themselves. I knew that Sister Kathleen was thinking of that, and keeping it to herself so as not to make me even more terrified. I felt as if a huge weight had descended on my shoulders. It was Maddy's whole life that was in hideous danger, not her GCSE results.

'I want to talk to her,' Sister Kathleen said. 'I want to have a quiet talk with her and make up my own mind. But it might be hard to arrange. She wasn't pleased to see me last Friday evening. I don't think I can go round to the Turners' house again and I don't think Maddy would come to me, if I asked her straight out. You and Jef will have to think of a way. Don't be too frightened, Robs. This may turn out to be nothing very much. We may be frightening ourselves over nothing.'

I felt that my cheeks were sticky-wet, and wiped my eyes. I'd been crying without realising it. 'Poor Steve. Isn't there anything you can do for him?'

'We've found him a flat,' she told me sadly. 'He's managing there, with a lot of support. But I don't think he'll stay.' She shook her head. 'We're dealing with Maddy now. We're going to help Maddy. Here.' She gave me a piece of paper, with two phone numbers neatly written on it. 'That's our numbers. The second one's the red phone, for emergencies only. We say that so that nobody's left stranded in a crisis while someone else is having a nice chat. Call me when you've fixed things up.'

Seven

*T*HE MARQUEE WAS UP IN THE WILD PARK. IT WAS
 striped blue and white, with little yellow and red
flags whisking round the top of the central pole. It stood
on the lawns looking stranded, like someone who's come
along to a party in fancy dress and found everyone else in
their ordinary clothes. The Bradfield Festival had always
been a small, quiet affair: mostly music, some plays,
some talks by slightly famous people who'd written travel
books or been on boring TV programmes. There was the
Co-op fête, but no funfair, because that would lower
Bradfield's tone. My parents used to take me to the
concerts, which I didn't enjoy because I knew they were
only doing it out of duty. The Marquee idea was new,
like the big banners hanging over the streets, and the
posters in shop windows. I hadn't thought about it
before, but probably the change dated from Ms Ridgemont-Brown's arrival. She and her confederate, Andrew
Shine, had conspired to wake the town up. They'd
wakened up more than they'd bargained for, when they
opened the Powerhouse.

When I talked to Jef I found that he alternated between
believing that Maddy was possessed by the ghost of
Sophie Raeburn, and being convinced she was having a
nervous breakdown. When I tried to hint that there might
be something nastier than sad Sophie invading Maddy's
mind, he brushed the idea aside. He said one ghost was
enough. We talked about getting her to see Sister

Kathleen, and decided the best thing to do was call a *Hajetu* rehearsal.

'Make it Wednesday,' I said. On that Wednesday evening my mother and my father were both going to be away. Dad was at a conference somewhere. Mum would be working so late (she worked for a TV station) she'd stay down in London for the night, as she sometimes did. I didn't know what would happen when Sister Kathleen tried to talk to Maddy. But I was sure I didn't want Mum or Dad arriving in the middle of it: dangling the car keys and telling me the BMW was on a double yellow line and could I please hurry …

This was on Monday morning. He met me at lunchtime and told me it was fixed up. He'd managed to catch Maddy on the way out of one of her exams.

'What was she like?' I asked.

We were walking round the playing field. People were sunbathing, splatted on the grass with their clothes hiked up and peeled down, like victims of some awful catastrophe.

'Like nothing,' he said. 'Oh, she's not better. She's not our Maddy, it's as bad as ever. The worst thing is, she doesn't seem to know anything's wrong. But you remember we'd agreed to lay off *Hajetu* until the twenty-second, when we'll both be clear of exams? I thought I'd have to explain madly. I was going to say I was desperate for a break, I badly needed to use some different mental muscles, I was running stir-crazy. I didn't need to. She said, "Oh, yes." I said, "Six o' clock on Wednesday then?" She said "Yes," again, and walked off. That was the whole conversation. It was like talking to a Barbie doll, Robs. Her eyes didn't move. Her face, it's still Maddy's face, but –'

'I know,' I whispered.

In a way it was lucky that it was exam time. People doing their GCSEs weren't really at school any more.

They came in for their papers and went home again. If any teachers noticed Maddy wasn't like her usual self, they'd put it down to the obvious.

'I'll tell Sister Kathleen.'

Jef laughed. 'Oh, Sister Kathleen. Hey, did you notice the new politically-correct term for the departed: *people who have died*, she said, do you remember that? We can't talk about spooks any more. We'll have to talk about the "corporeally challenged". I suppose the correct term for what's happened to Maddy is a "conflict of physical occupancy situation with the corporeally challenged."'

'Oh, shut up Jef.'

He stopped walking and looked at me with a sore, rueful smile.

'You sounded just like Maddy when you said that.'

'*Please stop it.*'

'Okay.' He patted my shoulder awkwardly. I thought of Steve Wakefield, big brother to Mike; and to Sophie Raeburn. 'You tell Sister K she'd better be there.' He laughed again, more naturally. 'You know something strange? I'm fine in the exams. I get my nose down and I do the stuff, churn it out question by question, no problem. It's between the papers that I think of Maddy, and it does my head in.'

I told Solange I was going to the Powerhouse to rehearse, and I'd call myself a taxi home if it was late. She didn't make any difficulties. I set out early on that Wednesday evening, into the unknown. I was leaving behind fourteen-year-old Roberta Hayward: quiet girl, talented young pianist, clever in some ways, immature in others. She walked out of our house with me, into the warm leafy sunshine of our suburban street; and she vanished, never to be seen again.

The Powerhouse was ready for the exhibition. Some of the projects had been moved down from the stage and grouped around the entrance. The tables and chairs were set up in the coffee bar, the ziggurat of miniature worlds was standing in the middle of them. It was lucky we weren't seriously going to rehearse, because there wasn't enough space.

Jef was admiring it all, while Sister Kathleen fidgeted with last minute touches.

'Looking good!' he declared: and then pulled a ball-just-smashed-the-window little boy face. 'No thanks to us three, eh? Sister Kathleen, I'm a useless dork at apologies, so let me say this before I lose my nerve.' He folded his hands in front of him and intoned, in a Christopher Robin squeak. 'We are very, very sorry that we spoilt your Residency with our dumb techno-thrash and our brainless dabbling in the occult. You didn't deserve us. What more can I say?'

I was glad he'd said it. I hoped she'd understand the Christopher Robin act was something he couldn't help. There was no need to worry. She'd come to know Jef, somehow. She smiled broadly. 'Ye're not to blame, but thank you anyway. Take three lively young people, add a spooky old building and a tragic secret … It was my own fault. I don't know what I *should* have done when I heard Dave Ramsey's story. But keeping my mouth shut was not the answer.'

'QED' agreed Jef, grimly. 'D'you think she's not going to show?'

It was getting late: and our Maddy was always so punctual. 'I'll make a cup of tea,' offered Sister Kathleen. Inevitably.

As she headed for the kitchen, Maddy came through the front doors. She was humming a tune, and smiling a little bright smile. She was dressed in her pink leather skirt, with a shiny mauve shirt and black tights. The black tights were an odd touch with that outfit. But seeing her in the flesh, I couldn't believe what I'd been believing. How could my friend be possessed by a demon? I didn't know if it was Maddy who was going mad, or me.

Sister Kathleen quietly took herself off, out of sight.

'What's the matter?' Maddy asked chirpily. 'Why haven't you started setting up? Come on you guys, let's get going!'

'Look, Maddy: I don't know about rehearsing. We ... Can we talk, for a moment?'

'Jef!' exclaimed Maddy, making her eyes wide and shocked. 'We don't have time to *talk!* This is a rehearsal!'

She jumped into action, chattering about how great it was going to be to play in the Festival, and how much she was looking forward to our big night ... It sounded completely fake. She sounded like someone acting the part of Maddy – popular, fun-loving Maddy Turner – in a bad soap opera. Jef gave up. He glanced at me with a resigned shrug, and began to set up. There was nothing for it. We'd have to go through with this 'rehearsal'. I didn't know how I was going to survive it. She surely couldn't be possessed by a demon, but she wasn't our Maddy. She soon left the set up to us, while she swopped her pink skirt for the dragonfly-dress: a stiff gauzy tutu, laced with fibre optics and decorated with squiggles of dayglo colour. She clowned around doing high kicks, until she kicked one of the miniature immersions out of its niche in the ziggurat.

I went to pick up the pieces. It had been a garden scene. There'd been a little china doll, out watering the twisted-tissue paper flowers with a tiny red watering can. She was broken into pathetic fragments. I hadn't the courage even to look at Maddy. She was there beside me, smiling, when I stood up. 'Oh well,' she said, blithely. 'Never mind.' She took the box from me, and dumped it in a waste basket.

Then we tried to rehearse. Me on the keyboards and the colour desk: Jef and Maddy singing and dancing. It was a disaster. Maddy was losing the tune, losing herself, forgetting what she was singing: and Jef was helpless, because he didn't know what she'd do next. She was swopping from one routine to another, as if someone was pushing buttons at random on her remote control. I tried to keep my eyes pinned to my keyboard. I saw an old prompt-list taped there, from weeks ago. It looked like the one Maddy had found in the undercroft, and reverently preserved as a relic of Sophie. I felt sick.

In our third attempted number she broke off in the middle of a phrase and wandered away. She started prowling around the Residency projects. There was a piece that was like a big drum, on three tall angled legs. The drum part was doughnut shaped. You ducked inside it and stood up, so your head was in the hole in the doughnut. Then you pressed a switch and the drum began to spin. You could control the speed, changing what you saw from a round of moving pictures to spinning arcs of smeared-out colour. Maddy stood with her head inside this moving drum, laughing crazily.

That was it. I looked at Jef, and he looked at me. He peeled off the Paintbox Pickup from his throat and dropped it on my desk.

'Okay,' he announced. 'We're going to take a break.'

Maddy was trying to pull a papier-mâché leaping panther from its stand. Suddenly she noticed the silence. 'Hey, is the rehearsal over? Then I'm going home!'

She didn't seem to think of changing, she just headed for the doors. Jef stood in her way. 'No,' he said. 'You're staying. We need to talk.'

I couldn't see Maddy's face. She didn't speak, but I saw Jef going very white. After a moment her shoulders lifted casually, and she strolled off to mess with something else. Jef seemed to steady himself. He took out a paper tissue and wiped his forehead.

Sister Kathleen came down from the studio area. She motioned us, with a jerk of her chin, to join her at one of the coffee bar tables. The three of us sat quietly. The evening sunlight in the hall seemed unnaturally bright and glaring on all those white walls; and the silence was intense. After a minute or two Maddy came over. She didn't comment on Sister Kathleen's sudden appearance. She sat, and smiled.

It was horrible to be near her. When she'd turned up, I had really hoped that my crazy fears were going to be swept away. I thought she was my friend Maddy again – maybe behaving a bit strangely, maybe suffering from a breakdown ... But it wasn't like that, nothing like that. I was *afraid*. There was no obvious reason for the way I felt, she hadn't grown fangs. There was only the subtle wrongness of her face, and the flat look in those Barbie-doll eyes. *Is this what being with a mad person is like?* I wondered. How could I know? I looked at Jef. I could tell from his strained, shocked face that he was feeling the same as me.

'Maddy,' said Sister Kathleen, gently. 'I want to have a word with you.'

A subtle change came over Maddy's expression. 'I've no objection!'

Her voice sounded odd, soft and sort of soppy. She changed her position a little, setting her feet primly together and making as if to smooth a longish skirt over her knees (though she was still wearing the tutu). She patted her hair, plumping it up at the back of her neck in a silly, fussy manner. I didn't know what was going on. It was as if Maddy was imitating someone, but I didn't know who.

Sister Kathleen did. I saw her stiffen, I saw her brace herself against a horrible shock.

'Dear Jesus, Kathleen,' said Maddy, in that same soft voice. This time I noticed the Irish accent. 'What a sight you look with that haircut.'

Sister Kathleen's red cheeks turned bloodless. Then she seemed to steady herself, like Jef when he'd stopped

—— 148 ——

Maddy from leaving. 'So, you found out about my sister, did you? Well, I suppose it was no great secret for a determined girl like you. But it's not kind of you to imitate her, Maddy. You're not well, are you. Will you tell me how you're feeling? Let us try to help you?'

'There's nothing wrong with me, Kathleen. I'm grand.'

'You are not Mary,' said Sister Kathleen, sternly. 'Stop that fooling.'

Jef and I stared at each other. I think we were both wondering whether Sister Kathleen was starting to imagine things. Maddy had not been there when Sister Kathleen told us about her sister. She must have found out some other way. But how? I was sure neither of us had told her. Then Maddy, only it wasn't Maddy, turned to look directly at Sister Kathleen, and spoke in a different voice. 'You are right. I am not Mary,' she said. That was all ... I hear those words sometimes, in nightmares. I can't describe what was wrong with her voice and face. But there was no way, from that moment, that anyone could have believed she was putting on an act, or playing the fool.

Then Sister Kathleen tried to talk with her. I think she'd had a lot of experience of talking to people in a poor state of mental health. She was very gentle, but sort of relentless. She would not allow Maddy to pretend there was nothing wrong. She went on and on, quietly chatting, asking about the exams, talking about her exhibition: but always coming back to Maddy herself, and the seances, and how she felt about them. Jef and I hardly spoke at all. I kept thinking we ought to go away and leave Sister Kathleen to it. We didn't seem to be doing anything to help. But whenever I caught her eye, trying to suggest this, she shook her head a little. So we stayed.

Maddy's defences never showed a sign of cracking. She pretended to be Mary, and made cruel little remarks.

Or she laughed crazily, or she reported all the nasty things Jef had ever muttered behind Sister Kathleen's back; and came up with a few more. But Sister Kathleen was determined not to give up. I saw (feeling suddenly older, as if I'd rushed through ten years in a few minutes) that it was because of her sister. She'd failed to save Mary. She *had* to rescue Maddy … I don't know how long this phase went on. The big windows began to grow dim.

'It's getting dark,' said Maddy.

Jef started to get up, to turn on the lights: but at the same moment we heard a rattle of rain against the glass, and a noisy gust of wind. The fine weather had broken. Sister Kathleen lifted her hand to stop him.

'What does that mean to you, Maddy?' she asked.

'It was dark that night. That other night. It was hot, but dark. There was a storm.'

'And then what happened, Maddy?'

'I am not Maddy,' she whispered. It was a new voice. Not horrible this time, but faint and sweet: I knew I'd heard that voice before.

Again Jef tried to jump up. Sister Kathleen put a hand on his arm, holding him back. Maddy suddenly began to cry. She buried her face in her hands and started to rock to and fro in her chair, sobbing very quietly, smothering the noise; like a child afraid she's going to get hit again if someone hears her crying. 'I can't stand this life,' she whimpered. 'Nobody loves me, my Mummy doesn't love me. I want to be someone else, don't call me Sophie. I want to go home but I can't, I can't ever go home. I wish I was dead, oh I wish I was dead.'

We three were very still. Maddy rocked in her chair, talking in dead Sophie's voice. It was getting darker. I felt a change in the space around me. I could see and hear nothing different, but it felt as if there were a lot of people near me. Our rainy night was cool, but I was too

—— 150 ——

warm. I could smell incense, mingled with the dust and dirt of an empty building. I could hear throbbing music, a raw bass beat. I could almost see the people now. People in fancy dress, with painted faces: jostling each other, holding bottles and plastic beakers, breaking into formless dance. I felt the way I'd felt at our last seance. I couldn't move. I couldn't cry out, couldn't ask Jef or Sister Kathleen if they too were seeing the ghosts.

Maddy stood up. She walked towards the stage. I wanted to shout *Don't let her!*, because I knew this was terribly wrong. But I couldn't.

I couldn't move, but Jef was getting very restless. Since the darkness gathered he'd been shifting about, obviously desperate to do something. Suddenly he spoke. 'This is doing no good,' he cried. 'Can't you see, Maddy isn't crazy. She's possessed. You're going to have to believe in ghosts, Sister. Sophie Raeburn is here. That's *Sophie*. She's taken over. We have to accept that, or we'll never get Maddy back.'

At the foot of the stone steps Maddy turned and looked back, with a sad, grateful smile, her face a pale glimmer in the gloom.

I wanted to shout, 'No, no, don't believe it. It's lying.' But no words came.

'Stay here,' ordered Jef, 'Let me talk with her.'

I think it was the bravest thing he'd ever done. I knew he was as terrified as I was myself. But up he went, for Maddy's sake.

It was hot in the dark hall. Hot and late. There were flaring torches in the sconces along the walls, threatening to set fire to the whimsical decorations; but the flamelight only made more confusion. It was hard to see what was going on up on the stage. The noise of the music was raw and harsh yet somehow thin as well, as if there was nothing under the surface. Between pulsing walls of white light I saw two black figures, two masked men playing electric guitars. There was a girl in front of them, very still in contrast to their prancing, very slight and pale: a pitiful, vulnerable figure. I heard her singing faintly *Oh Mister D'Eath* ... I knew that she had a maggot in her brain. It was telling her to kill herself. I tried to put my hands over my eyes. I didn't want to see what I was going to be made to see. I felt rushing in on me that moment, the terrible moment that had been trapped here for so many years, waiting to be enacted again. I heard Jef's voice saying gently: 'Sophie, it's over. You can rest now. You can leave Maddy and go in peace.'

Maddy was sitting cross-legged on the stage, Jef crouched beside her. Her head was bowed, her hands hidden in her lap, in the stiff gauze of her dancing dress. There was nothing else, the vision of the long ago night was only in my mind.

'Oh, Jesus!' gasped Sister Kathleen. She jumped up from her seat, and rushed to the stage. Then I saw what she had seen and I ran after: screaming 'Jef! She's got a knife!'

Sister Kathleen raced up the stone steps and launched herself at Maddy. I don't know exactly what happened next. There was a struggle, Maddy broke free and ran away. Jef was kneeling, holding his left arm in his right: and there was blood everywhere. One of Sister Kathleen's craft knives was lying there, its razor sharp slanting blade covered in red.

She had slashed Jef's wrist wide open. It was bleeding incredibly. Sister Kathleen grabbed both my hands, and slammed them on the inside of his left elbow. 'Press hard!' she ordered. *'Don't let go.'* She rushed off, and returned instantly with a length of fabric. In a moment she'd applied a rough tourniquet. She sent me for the first aid kit that was kept in the kitchen. By the time I came back Jef was lying down, protesting groggily that he was fine, he was perfectly all right. And then he fainted.

'Is he going to be all right?' I pleaded.

'I'll have to take him to the hospital,' decided Sister Kathleen grimly, when she'd bandaged him as best she could. 'Thank God those wastrels on our estate left us the car.'

'But what about Maddy?'

Sister Kathleen looked around desperately. There was no sign of her.

'I'll have to call someone to come and deal with her.'

'I'll stay until they come.'

'You will not! Robs, I hope to God what happened with the knife was an accident. In fact I'm sure it was. But I can't leave you alone with Maddy in such a state.' She looked at Jef. 'I have to get him to a doctor!' She gave a sort of groan. 'Oh, this is all my fault. I'm a stupid auld woman, biting off more than I can chew.'

I could see how torn she was, how she was trying frantically to think of a way to deal with this situation: and finding no answers.

'You've to come with us down to the phone box on the road,' she decided. 'We'll leave this place locked behind us. Then you're to ring that "red phone" number I gave you. You have it with you?' I nodded quickly. 'Tell Sister Monica or Sister Margaret Mary there's been an accident. Tell them I've had to take someone to hospital, and that there's a young girl here very distressed. Tell them to come here fast. Then you wait by the phone box until they arrive, and tell them all you know. They may need to call someone else, depending on how Maddy is when they get here. Say I'll call, and get back as soon as I can.'

It was raining hard. We helped Jef out to the forecourt between us, and arranged him in the back seat. Then we locked up, I got into the front and we drove to the phone box at the Wild Park gates. Sister Kathleen gave me her keys.

I stood in the booth, the receiver in my hand, and watched her drive away.

Then I went out again into the rain, and walked quickly back to the Powerhouse.

I let myself in. There was still no sign of Maddy. I went to the office beside the kitchen, where there was a telephone. I sat on the office chair, my hands over my mouth. My hands were so cold! As if I'd dipped them in ice. I picked up the phone and called Solange. I told her Maddy had invited me to go home and sleep over. I said I'd forgotten to explain this earlier because I'd been in a hurry, but Mum and Dad knew all about it. She was cross and suspicious, but in the end she said okay. Then I called the Turners. I told Maddy's mother that Maddy was going to come home with me because I was feeling ill, and she might stay the night, as otherwise I'd be alone with only Solange and Jerry ... Of course that was all right. Maddy's Mum trusted her completely: everybody trusted Maddy. Her Mum might have wondered why I was talking to her, and not Maddy herself. But Flick and Eddie started having a screaming fight while we were talking, so she had to ring off.

Why did I make these phone calls, instead of the call I was supposed to make? Because I knew what Sister Kathleen meant when she said *We may have to call someone to deal with her*. She thought Maddy had gone completely out of her mind, like Mary long ago. She thought Maddy was crazy, and probably dangerous. *Someone* meant the police, or the men in white coats. I thought of Maddy fighting with big policemen, struggling and screaming. I couldn't bear it. Maybe the people who took charge of her would have been much more gentle than I imagined. But I saw Maddy in a straitjacket. I thought of them putting a rubber gag in her mouth, pumping her full of 'brain-death medication'. I thought they'd have to do that, if she was violent. And I knew that if what I believed was true, treating her as if she was crazy could only make things much worse. I couldn't let it happen.

If Sister Kathleen had been convinced that Maddy was possessed by an evil spirit, perhaps she would have acted differently. But though she knew we'd been playing stupid games with the supernatural, in a place that had a nasty atmosphere and grim history, she didn't know enough to make her believe that. Steve Wakefield had never told her about the creature he and Mike and Sophie had conjured into being. I had told no one about the rat, the little animal-thing with bright, evil eyes. And anyway, Sister Kathleen didn't want to believe the worst. I could understand that … But I knew she was a wise woman, and I believed she had told me the truth about fighting demons. Faith and courage, love and prayer. I didn't feel as if I had any courage, but I had faith in Sister Kathleen. I would give it a try.

The Powerhouse was ablaze with lights now, but I took the big torch from the store cupboard, just in case. Then I went to look for Maddy.

I checked the kitchen and the rest of that passageway first. I locked those rooms and went into the hall. Everything was very still, except for the doughnut-drum which was still turning, slowly and lazily. It was so bright, so many lights. I would never have thought anyone could be as frightened as I was, amidst so much light and whiteness.

'Maddy?'

I looked behind the coffee bar counter, in case she was hiding under there. I went through into the unused craft-rooms, beyond the right-hand door. These were all completely empty, except for some art stores, and a lot of big empty cardboard boxes. The boxes were bad to deal with, even worse than the counter. I had to go right up to them to see inside; afraid every second that she would burst out and leap at me. I'd locked the kitchen, and left the bloodied craft knife in there: but I knew she could have found another one. Sister Kathleen didn't keep her tools locked up.

'Maddy?'

I opened the undercroft door and peered in. There was no sign of Maddy among the tainted relics. I climbed up on to the stage. Sister Kathleen's immersions loomed around me. My biggest fear was that Maddy would get to the fusebox, and I'd suddenly be plunged in darkness. No … my biggest fear was that I would find her body. The other girls had killed themselves. I knew she hadn't meant to hurt Jef. The knife had been meant for herself. There was a maggot in her brain. I remembered how it had felt to stand in the cold patch. I thought of Maddy trapped in that terrible state of mind. She couldn't escape, because the thing that drew out the badness and fed on it was *inside her.* How I wished to God I had told them all, long ago … But it would have done no good. They wouldn't have believed me.

I leaned on the shell of the 'Easter Rising'. My knees were trembling so I could hardly walk. I saw the letters on Alanna's alphabet cards, spelling out the words of the message. GO NOW, OR GO NEVER. We didn't understand. We didn't know it was a warning.

She was inside one of the immersions. As I stood trembling, wondering how I could make myself go on with the search, I heard a small noise like tearing paper. I looked into the artifical mound that was called 'My Heart Is Like A Singing Bird': and there was Maddy, squatting on the floor. The inside of 'My Heart' was painted in pink and red, shading into green near the floor. The colour was covered by a layer of clear plastic that had all kinds of pretty Victorian oddments set into it: greeting cards with lacy edges, pictures of birds and roses, garlands of daisies and young women in crinolines and poke bonnets. Maddy had a woodworking chisel in her hand. She'd been hacking at the clear layer, to get at the souvenirs. When I looked in she was tearing up a Victorian valentine. She stared at me, and the thing that was inside her smiled.

I said, 'Hello Maddy. *Maddy* I'm talking to you. It's me, Robs,' (I couldn't stop my voice from shaking). 'The others have gone. I know what's happened. I know about the creature. You're not going mad. It's real. Steve and Mike and Sophie conjured it here. It got into Sophie, and then the other two girls. It made them all kill themselves, and since then it's been waiting for another chance. I saw it at the seance. That's when it got into your mind –'

Next moment, I found myself plastered up against the shell of the 'Immortality' immersion. I'd dropped my torch. Nothing had touched me, but I felt as if someone had punched me in the stomach, and boxed my ears at the same time. My head was ringing.

But I felt triumphant. I had won the first round. I had made it show itself. It knew it couldn't fool me any more. I forced myself to go back. I couldn't stand, my legs were shaking too much. So I crawled, into the entrance to 'My Heart'.

Maddy held the chisel warningly. I reminded myself that Sister Kathleen thought I could do this. Faith and courage, love and prayer. Like lifesaving. If you're the only person there, *you have to try*.

'Maddy, I'm talking to *you*, Maddy. We can beat it. I know we can. It's only a stupid little monkey-thing that likes munching on bad feelings. Sophie was very miserable, the other two girls didn't know what was going on. They had no chance, they were sitting ducks. You're different, you can fight back. And you have me. I'm with you.'

'How do you know,' it asked, with a horrible, uncertain slowness, 'that Maddy is not miserable?' I could tell that it was her, it was *Maddy*, fighting the demon to speak.

I don't know if I can call the creature *evil*. That makes it sound human, as if it knew what it was doing and could stop and do something else if it wanted. It wasn't like that. Maybe only human beings can do evil things. This wasn't a person, it was an appetite. It was eating Maddy's mind, eating her alive from the inside, and this was its natural state. It could do nothing else but destroy. I began to shake harder. Yet I knew that something was changing ... It was Maddy who had asked that question. The demon was no longer in complete control.

'Because ... you are good, Maddy,' I managed to whisper. 'You are good to people. You like to be kind. That's why we all like you. Maybe you have troubles I don't know about, but if you have they don't make you hate yourself. Deep down you're all right with life. I am sure of that.'

It would be different, I thought, (shaking horribly) if the thing had got hold of me.

I was wrong about it losing control. Maddy's face contorted, with a savage look of malice. I started seeing pictures in my mind. I won't describe them. You can see pictures of horrible suffering any day, just watch the news on TV. I knew that I was seeing what it was showing Maddy, that it was making her join it in feeding, making her share its appetite. I tried to fight back, but for a while I was lost. I had to curl up in a ball, hiding my face, while the horrors ran through me. But I didn't go away. I stayed there.

I don't know how long that went on. At last I woke up as if from a nightmare, cold and sweaty. When it saw my eyes open, it leapt at me. I felt something hard bang onto my right hand, between the fingers and thumb. It had stabbed me with the chisel. I struggled and fought: with Maddy or whatever was inside her. The chisel went flying, and Maddy ran off across the stage, down into the hall. I jumped up, clutching my hand, and ran after. Where was Maddy? Where could she be? The door to the undercroft was standing ajar. I must have forgotten to lock it again, or else it had come open by itself.

'*Oh no,*' I muttered. '*Please not in there ...*' But I went inside. The light from the hall behind me showed a dim figure, sitting on the wicker sofa: where the ghost of Sophie Raeburn had appeared.

I think I used up the last of my power to be afraid, as I stepped into that gloom. The figure didn't move. I didn't go near it at first. I collected some of the candles that were still lying about on the floor, left there since the night when Sister Kathleen had broken up the last seance. Not the black ones ... I put them on the table and lit them. The purple skull was there, grinning cheekily. It had burned down so that one of the eye-sockets was half melted: it looked as if the skull was winking. I thought of Steve and Mike and Sunny and how safe they had felt in their den, before everything went wrong.

Maddy sat there, her face slack and her arms hanging loosely, like a machine switched off. I had the horrible thought that this was the way she had been, any time no one was looking at her, since Thursday night.

But I knew that inside, deep inside, she was fighting for her life.

'Maddy, I'm here,' I said. 'I'm right beside you.'

I sat on one of the peacock chairs. The chisel cut was bleeding a bit, but it didn't hurt yet. I found a wad of grubby tissue in the pocket of my jeans and held it tight over the place.

'Maddy?'

She said, barely moving her lips ... '*stay.*'

'Oh God,' I whispered. Was that Maddy's true voice, or another trick? 'I'll stay.'

The room seemed to grow very stuffy. The thing that looked out of Maddy's eyes had reached me now. I felt that a great weight was crushing me, and then it was through my defences. It squeezed itself like a squirming leech, forcing its way between the muscle and bone of my soul. It stuck there like pitch: sucking at the marrow. I thought of Sister Kathleen's 'Easter Rising' immersion:

and the poison in the heart of everything beautiful, everything we most desire. I knew why Steve and Mike and Sunny had wanted to conjure a spirit to serve them. They longed to be famous. Ordinary life wasn't enough for them, they wanted more. They wanted to get out of Bradfield, escape from all the ties that bind. They were hungry in a way that normal people can't understand ...

I can't tell you how horrible, how completely horrible this time was.

Yet all the while I was merely sitting beside my friend – the two of us strangely silent in the flickering candlelight. There was no sign of the struggle that was going on, no sign at all. I didn't know if seconds or minutes or hours were passing. I didn't say any words: but I believe I did pray. I remembered Sister Kathleen saying *ask, just ask*. Then I felt I couldn't even do that any more. I was down to bare endurance. I knew that if this went on I would have to give in. But from moment to moment, I kept hanging on.

Please, I thought. *Please help us* ...

And there came a moment when I knew that I was going to win. The crushing weight left me. I could hear Maddy's breathing, soft and low in the quiet dark ...

When I woke up it was morning, I was still in the peacock chair, but someone had tucked a fleecy-lined jacket over me. I opened my eyes and stretched. I looked at the jacket – which I thought I recognised – and wondered how it had got there. Maddy was lying on the sofa, on her side, covered by a mangy satin quilt. I didn't want to disturb her, but when I moved to stand up (I was very stiff), she woke. My heart gave a great thump and jump of relief. It was *Maddy*, herself again. She held out her hand. I took it in my left hand – the right one was a stiff fist clutched around a wad of bloodied tissue. We smiled at each other. Maddy stood up. I followed her, out into the hall. There, lying fast asleep on an uncomfortable looking bed made of six green metal chairs, was Sister Kathleen.

Maddy laid her finger to her lips. We crept quietly to the double doors, and opened them. The rain was over. It was about six o'clock on a fine summer morning. There were birds singing in the Wild Park, and the air was fresh as dew. She didn't say anything and neither did I. How could we ever describe what had happened?

We'd find out later that Sister Kathleen had tried to call the Drop-In Centre from the hospital, but she hadn't been able to get through. She'd called Jef's parents. As soon as his dad turned up she'd rushed back to the Powerhouse. She had found the place all lit up, but no sign of nuns, ambulances or squad cars. I had her keys, and she was locked out. By then it was after midnight. She'd had to go and knock up the caretaker. When he'd let her in, she'd found me and Maddy sleeping peacefully in the undercroft.

But the sorting out and the explanations came later.

'It was like a nightmare ...' I whispered.

'Yes,' said Maddy. 'It was a bad dream. It's gone now.'

We stood listening to the birdsong, and breathing the sweet air.

Maddy squeezed my hand. 'We'll have to wake her,' she said at last. 'So we can all go home. Shall I make some tea?' And we laughed.

ii

We had to invent a story to cover what had happened at the Powerhouse that night. We kept it as simple as possible. We said we'd been helping Sister Kathleen do some last minute work on one of her immersions, when we'd had an accident. I'd hurt my hand, but Jef had cut himself so badly that he had to be rushed to hospital. In the confusion Maddy and I had been left behind, locked in. We'd tried to phone the caretaker, but we must have been using the wrong number. Without telling Maddy, I had phoned up Mrs Turner and Solange with my fake stories, in a misguided attempt to keep people from worrying. Then we two had been talking, waiting for Sister Kathleen and not realising the time, and finally fallen asleep.

That was our story. Sister Kathleen backed us up, and there was no aftermath. Sister Kathleen swathed the ruined immersion 'My Heart Is Like A Singing Bird' in canvas, taped it up and told anyone who asked she was having a major rethink about that one.

Maddy seemed to be fine, perfectly fine. She said she didn't remember much about the past few days, except that she'd been feeling terribly miserable for no good reason: and somehow she couldn't talk to anyone. I thought the fact that Sister Kathleen helped us to cover up, and no longer seemed worried about Maddy's mental health, was an admission that what had happened to Maddy was no ordinary breakdown. But she never said so. However, she kept a close eye on us all for the rest of her stay in Bradfield. I think that by the time she left she was satisfied that we were all okay.

We three never went back to the Powerhouse, except to fetch our stuff.

Our set at the Festival Finale in the Marquee was a big success. Jef's arm was still in bandages and my hand still had a big impressive plaster, which gave us an emergency-room look that we played up to in our costumes. The Marquee was packed, with all our friends and most of the rest of the under-thirties in town. They loved us. They danced and cheered and sang along – whether or not they knew the words, or had any grasp of the tune. But Maddy was their favourite. She wore her shimmery snakeskin jeans, and had firefly lights in her dark hair that flashed all the colours of the rainbow.

For me it was one of those performances that is technically fine but not great on personal satisfaction. Maddy's voice was lovely as ever, Jef's songs as sharp and funny. But to me they both sounded tired. We hadn't talked much about the ordeal we'd been through. I think we'd all decided, following Sister Kathleen's lead, that the best thing was to let it go, let it vanish and heal without too many questions. But I was still feeling jaded, and hollow inside. I suspected the others must feel worse: they'd had their exams to cope with as well.

We escaped from our last encore and vacated the stage, leaving our set-up (what luxury!) to be dismantled by the Festival roadies. Maddy and Jef changed out of their costumes. I wiped off my make-up. The night was yet young, the show was still going on. They were dancing to disco music now. We left the Marquee, walked away from the noise, and sat down on the grass. Maddy folded her arms round her knees. She sighed.

'There's something I have to tell you.'

'Go on,' suggested Jef. 'I had my fly undone all through the set. Break it to me gently.'

But we knew she wasn't joking.

'I want to give up *Hajetu*.'

We were silent, though not from shock. I think we'd known it was coming. 'At least for a while,' she added, trying to soften the blow. But we knew she meant forever.

'I'm very tired,' she whispered sadly.

Jef put his arm round her shoulders. After a moment, so did I.

So that was the end of *Hajetu*: me and Jef and Maddy sitting with our arms around each other in the summer night, thinking of what might have been. We had never looked beyond this June, and we'd been right. Everything ends, everything passes. Maybe *Hajetu* couldn't have lasted much longer, anyway. Life goes on. 'It could have been worse,' said Jef. 'We reached a peak, you know. We had some perfect moments. That's enough.'

The stars were very bright, above the lights of our home town. We sat and watched them for a while, and talked about ordinary things. Then Maddy said she had to go home.

And that's the end of the story. *Hajetu* broke up. Jef did brilliantly in his GCSEs, Maddy not so good. Everybody was surprised and sorry for her, but the teachers said they knew she'd been getting stressed. She'd been working too hard, and she'd paid the price. She was ill with some kind of flu that summer, after the Festival. When she got better she went to college, where she retook some of her exams and did well. But she left after a year.

Jef is away at university, and isn't doing much music. Me, I'm at college. I'm still working with sound-to-light units. John Jeffries' type of instruments are no longer quirky prototypes. Better machines are being developed, and I'm composing for them. They say I'm good. I know I'm hungry for something. Maybe I'll be famous one day. Maddy has a job now. She isn't interested in performing anymore. It seems that wanting to be a pop-star was something she grew out of, the way people usually grow out of their teenage daydreams. I suppose most people who know her, even her parents, think she's having a normal happy life, and she simply turned out to be not very ambitious. But I remember Maddy, the bright flame. That midsummer morning when we stood together hand in hand after our terrible vigil, I thought I had saved her. And I did save her; or I helped her to save herself. But no one walks away unscathed from a fight like that. Her last performance with *Hajetu* was the final spark. A Maddy who could have been, the Maddy we all admired so much, was gone forever.

Why Maddy? Why didn't the demon pick on me? I spent a while afterwards wondering if she had some secret terrible trouble that had made her attractive as prey. But I don't think that was it. Sophie Raeburn was vulnerable because she was very unhappy. The other two girls were probably perfectly normal wannabe pop-stars. They just didn't know what hit them, so they hadn't a chance. Then I came along, but I was too scared: I shut my mind, I kept myself out of reach. Maddy's reaction was different. Right from the beginning, when she told us she was investigating a murder mystery, I think she knew she was dealing with something evil and strange. But she was brave and confident, and determined to find out the truth. That's why she took the risks she did, and that's how the demon managed to take control. Once it was in her mind, of course it found things to feed upon. We're all made the same. We all have our miseries and terrors: even people like Maddy.

I don't want anyone who reads this to get the idea that Maddy somehow deserved what happened, or that the demon got hold of her because she was weak. She walked into the monster's den, believing she couldn't be harmed. She was wrong, and she suffered for her mistake. But if she'd been anyone else but Maddy, I think there's a good chance neither of us would have survived that night.

There's one of Sister Kathleen Dunne's famous installations in the Bradfield Free Trade Gallery. It's the one called 'Immortality', where you stand in washes of gold, with shells and sand under your feet, and hear the voices of children mingled with the roaring of the mighty breakers on the shore. I'm glad the Gallery bought that one, and not 'Easter Rising'. And I'm glad it's in the Gallery. If it was kept in the other place I'd never see it. The Powerhouse, now known as The Source, is a flourishing performance venue, gallery and studio, but I don't go there. I don't believe it is haunted any more, but I spent enough time in that building one long, long summer night. I never want to go back.

I suppose this whole story could be told without the demon. I could say that I had a friend who had a sort of breakdown, and when she recovered she wasn't quite the same person. I could tell you that all the rest of it was just our imaginations. Some of the time I'm sure there was no more to it than that. But some of the time, especially if I go to the Gallery and visit Sister Kathleen's immersion, or if I'm listening to music that reminds me of *Hajetu*, I remember Maddy the way she was: and I know. And sometimes, especially if I'm alone and it's late at night, I watch in the corners of the room. I watch for shadows where no shadows should be. I watch for a sly movement, on the edge of the corner of my eye. I never see anything. I'm sure there's nothing there: only a scar on my memory, that refuses to fade. But that doesn't stop me looking.